P9-CQF-767

Ex-Library: Friends of
Lake County Public Library

Wheels Roll West

*Other Five Star Titles
by Wayne D. Overholser:*

Riders of the Sundowns
Chumley's Gold: A Western Duo
Nugget City
Gateway House: A Western Story
Rainbow Rider: A Western Trio
Outlaws

Wheels Roll West

A Western Duo

Wayne D. Overholser

Five Star • Waterville, Maine

LAKE COUNTY PUBLIC LIBRARY

3 3113 02173 5016

Copyright © 2002 by the Estate of Wayne D. Overholser

"Swampland Empire" first appeared as a four-part serial in
Ranch Romances (2nd October Number: 10/13/50—
2nd November Number: 11/24/50). Copyright © 1950
by Best Books, Inc. Copyright © renewed 1978 by
Wayne D. Overholser. Copyright © 2002 by the Estate of
Wayne D. Overholser for restored material.

"Wheels Roll West" first appeared as a four-part serial in
Ranch Romances (2nd March Number: 3/16/51—
3rd April Number: 4/27/51). Copyright © 1951
by Best Books, Inc. Copyright © renewed 1979 by
Wayne D. Overholser. Copyright © 2002 by the Estate of
Wayne D. Overholser for restored material.

All rights reserved.

Five Star First Edition Western Series.

Published in 2002 in conjunction with
Golden West Literary Agency.

Set in 11 pt. Plantin by Elena Picard.

Printed in the United States on permanent paper.

Library of Congress Cataloging-in-Publication Data

Overholser, Wayne D., 1906–
    [Swampland empire]
    Wheels roll West : a western duo / Wayne D. Overholser.
—1st ed.
        p. cm.
    "Five Star western"—T.p. verso.
    Contents: Swampland empire—Wheels roll West.
    ISBN 0-7862-3529-2 (hc : alk. paper)
    1. Western stories. I. Overholser, Wayne D., 1906–
Wheels roll West. II. Title.
    PS3529.V33 S93 2002
    813′.54—dc21   2002024353

Table of Contents

Swampland Empire

Chapter One

The town of Getalong was in Blue Lake Valley far down in the southeast corner of Oregon, but there wasn't a map in existence that showed it. The reason was simple. The map makers had never heard of it, for Getalong was less than a year old on this June day when Brad Wilder drove Cory Steele's wagon into town for supplies.

Brad had been whistling all the way in from the Steele place. He felt good, and he had a right to. Given two more years, or even one, and he'd be set. Then he was close enough to the store to recognize the two saddle horses racked in front, and the good humor in him died. One belonged to Whang Dollit, the other to Nick Bailey.

Brad pulled up in front of the store, gray eyes on the saloon door. Even a new country was likely to have its share of tough hands, and Whang Dollit filled the bill here. Not that he claimed to be tough. He didn't have to. It was written all over him, and some of that writing had rubbed off on young Bailey.

Brad tied the team, and went into the store. It was empty. Dollit and Bailey would be in the saloon. He went on along the rough pine counter to the back room, hoping he would find Tom Hildreth, the store owner, there. Before he had thrown in with Cory Steele and the wagon train a year ago, Brad would have gone out of his way to get into a fight just for the joy of the fighting, but this year had changed him. Cory had done that, Cory and his dark-eyed daughter, Jeanie.

Hildreth wasn't in the back room, so he'd have to be in the saloon. Brad walked back to the front door, hoping that Hildreth would hear him. He stood there for a time, looking across the valley, and for a moment he forgot Whang Dollit. Blue Lake Valley had everything that went into the making of a good cattle country—grass.

The worst thing about this country was the distance to a settlement, for it was stretching the truth a little to call Getalong a town. There was this one two-story building. The first floor consisted of the store on one side, a saloon on the other; the second was a single large room where the settlers held their dances. A shed stood behind the building, some corrals beside it, and there was a dwelling house to the east. That was Getalong, and Tom Hildreth owned it all.

Impatience grew in Brad. He swung back, and walked through the wall door into the saloon side of the building. He had no reason to think he'd have trouble with Dollit today, but sooner or later it would come. His dislike of the man was instinctive, and he had no illusion about how Dollit felt toward him.

Dollit and Nick Bailey were bellied up against the bar, two pine planks laid across a couple of whisky barrels. Hildreth stood behind the bar, a fat man with a shiny bald head and a great white beard that gave him the appearance of a benign Santa Claus. In a way he was exactly that, for he was giving credit to every settler in the valley except Cory Steele and Whang Dollit.

Hildreth said in his friendly way: "Howdy, Brad. This your drinking day?"

"No. I've got a list of stuff Jeanie wants."

Dollit grinned and winked at Hildreth. "I hear Jeanie don't like a man that drinks."

He was a squat man, a head shorter than Brad and fifty pounds heavier with a dark-jowled face that was always barren of good nature, even when he grinned as he was doing now. Whang Dollit's smiles never reached up into his eyes that were as black and shiny as chipped obsidian.

"Dollit," Brad said evenly, "you must have quite a time living with yourself."

"Cut it out," Hildreth broke in. "I'll get your stuff, Brad."

"No hurry, is there?" Dollit asked. "I've got a notion Nick here wants to say something."

Bailey had been staring at an empty whisky glass in his hand. He raised bloodshot eyes to Brad, scowling, then dropped his gaze again to his glass. "Not today, Whang."

"Why this is as good a day as any," Dollit said. "You need another drink." He reached for the bottle, and filled Bailey's glass. "A man who's losing his girl has got to keep his courage up."

"Cut it out, Dollit," Hildreth said again. "Go ahead with your drinking. I'll go fix Brad up."

"Slow down, Tom," Dollit said. "You're too fat to be hurrying around like this. Bad for your heart." He lifted paper and tobacco from his shirt pocket, gaze swinging to Brad. "Heard the news?"

Brad held his answer a moment, watching Bailey who was slowly turning his filled glass between thumb and forefinger. He was twenty-three, and more of a kid than he should have been at that age. Slender, high-strung, nervous, Nick Bailey was the kind who might blow up without warning. Now, filled with whisky and with Dollit's words

11

honing his jealousy to a fine edge, he might do the unexpected.

Dollit's big hands fisted. He said ominously: "I asked you a question, Wilder."

Still watching Bailey, Brad said: "No, I ain't heard no news."

"Well, there's news to hear, bucko," Dollit said as if pleased by the opportunity to tell it. "Just like I've been saying. A man ought to be sure that a piece of land is open for filing before he settles on it. You fools went along with Cory Steele with your eyes shut. Now you'll lose your places just like I figured."

"Well, what is this news?" Brad asked.

"What have I been saying all winter? I kept telling you this here valley had been taken over by the state as swampland. Now it's been sold to a cowman named Riley Rand. Where does that leave you and Cory Steele and the rest?"

"Where does it leave you," Brad demanded, "providing it's true?"

"It's true, all right," Dollit said with deep satisfaction. "I talked to Rand. His herd's down the trail, but he's in the valley. Camped below the south rim. He wasn't pleased when he got a look at our shacks. No, sir, he sure wasn't. Claims he bought fifty thousand acres, and that's all there is in this valley."

"Fifty thousand acres," Brad said slowly. "What kind of a cussed lie are you passing out, Dollit? There ain't five thousand acres of real swampland around the lake."

"No, there ain't," Dollit agreed, "but that don't make no never mind to the state or Riley Rand. The state wants a dollar and a quarter an acre, and Rand wants the range. He showed me an official map. The whole valley, tules and sagebrush and all, is marked with red S's. It's been called

12

swampland whether it's swamp or not, and he's got it."

Brad shoved his hat back with a thumb, glancing at Hildreth who was staring at Dollit as if uncertain whether to believe this or not. It could be true, for there had been similar rumors almost from the day the wagon train had reached the valley.

Cory Steele knew, as all of them knew, that large pieces of land in this part of Oregon had been turned over to the state by the federal government as swampland. The state, in turn, was selling it to cowmen who were driving their herds north from Nevada and California, but Cory had pointed out that at this late date anyone who wanted free land had to gamble.

The bulk of the good land had been homesteaded long ago. If a poor man wanted a home, he had to take what Uncle Sam had left to give. The valley was isolated, but there was water here, and in time a railroad would come. Or if it didn't, cattle could be pooled and driven south to the railroad at Winnemucca.

So, because Cory Steele was a persuasive man, they had gambled; they had built their cabins and turned their cattle into the lush grass around the lake and along the creek.

"You settled here, too," Brad said finally. "I asked where it left *you?*"

Dollit laughed. "Well, sir, I ain't worrying. I'll make some money. The way I look at it, we've got a little nuisance value, so I figure to hang and rattle until this Rand makes us a proposition."

"What kind of a proposition?" Hildreth asked.

"Hell, how would I know? I'll get something, though. Rand will have to send for a U.S. marshal to run us out. I figure it'll be cheaper if he buys us out just to get rid of us."

"Wouldn't be much," Hildreth said thoughtfully.

13

"No, but it'd be something."

"Not for anybody who planned to make a home here," Brad said curtly. "You gonna get me this stuff, Tom?"

"Sure, right away," Hildreth said. He turned and moved ponderously into the store.

Brad followed, and handed him the list Jeanie had made out. Hildreth scanned it. He shook his head. "I'm plumb out of canned tomatoes, Brad. I've got everything else."

"Then I guess she'll do without tomatoes."

"I sent a wagon out early in the spring," Hildreth said apologetically. "It ought to be in before long. How is Cory, Brad? I ain't heard lately."

"Poorly," Brad said. "It's been two months since that ornery cayuse threw him, but his leg ain't mending like it should, and he's got an appetite like a bird. Jeanie thought some tomatoes would go down pretty good."

"I'm sure sorry, Brad. I just ain't got a can."

Brad carried the supplies to the wagon as Hildreth set them out, and, when he was finished, he tossed a gold eagle on the counter. He asked: "You believe what Dollit said about this Riley Rand?"

Hildreth drew some silver dollars from his pocket and laid three of them down. "I'm afraid I do, Brad. He ain't got any reason for lying."

Brad pocketed the silver, thinking of Dollit who had drifted into the valley the fall after the wagon train had come. He had built a cabin, and that was all he had done. He hadn't put in a garden; he didn't own any cattle or chickens or pigs. Just a saddle horse and a pack animal, but he seemed to have money.

Until he had taken up with Nick Bailey, Dollit had been a friendless man, largely because he jeered at everyone for settling here. From the first he had prophesied the very thing he now said had happened. According to the gossip, he was on the dodge and the valley was a good place to stay for there was no lawman within a hundred miles. Now Brad wondered.

"I dunno," Brad said. "He's a scheming son-of-a-bitch. Maybe he's figured out something else."

"Maybe." Hildreth put his hands on the counter and leaned across it. "Brad, that Bailey boy worries me. He's drinking too much. Is it Jeanie?"

"Don't ask me," Brad said irritably. "He's got as much chance with her as anybody."

"Except that you're Cory's neighbor, and you've been helping 'em. Nick's been worse since Cory busted his leg."

"Well, what do you expect me to do, tell Jeanie to marry him?"

Hildreth shook his head. "No, but somebody's got to do something. He's been in love with her for a long time, Brad. He figures he's lost Jeanie, and he blames you." The store man gestured wearily. "Me, I blame Cory. He never liked Nick much. I've been thinking you might talk to Cory. Have him give the boy work. Have Jeanie invite him out for a meal. Do something before Nick goes plumb loco."

"I'll tell Cory," Brad said, and, turning, walked out.

Without intending to, Jeanie Steele made a man's heart do things. Brad and young Bailey weren't the only men in the valley who were in love with her, and Brad wasn't sure he had the inside track. He knew that Cory liked him, but that didn't help with Jeanie. She wasn't the kind who could be told by her father or anyone else who she had to marry.

Brad paused in front of the store to roll a smoke, his eyes on the long ridges of the Blue Mountains to the north as he thought of the first time he had seen Jeanie. He had been aimlessly riding north from Linkville along the east side of the Cascade Mountains, a drifter at twenty-five without a solid thought in his head. He had turned west to follow the Santiam Pass to the Willamette Valley when he had met the wagon train. Jeanie was riding with Cory up in front, a slim, dark-haired girl with a scattering of freckles across a pert nose and eager brown eyes that danced with anticipation.

Brad had never thought it would happen to him, this thing of falling in love with a girl the first time he saw her, but it had. He could have had his choice of a hundred girls. Brad Wilder had a way with girls, and he'd had little conscience about it. He'd taken them to dances, they'd flirted with him, he'd kissed them, and he'd ridden off without a second thought about the broken hearts that lay along his back trail. Then he'd seen Jeanie, and the pattern had been reversed.

They had camped that night on the Deschutes. He had sat up late with Cory Steele after the others had gone to bed, and he had listened to Cory talk about the future of Blue Lake Valley. Cory had seen it when he had come out this way a short time before, and, when he had gone back across the Cascades, he had sold everything he owned and talked his neighbors into coming with him.

"Look at you, Wilder," Cory had said. "You don't own nothing but a buckskin horse and a saddle and the clothes on your back. Where are you headed?"

"Why, I never thought much about it," Brad had answered.

"Then you'd better start thinking. A man shouldn't wait till it's too late to decide on what he's shooting at. I came near doing that. Tomorrow we're swinging over to the Crooked River to pick up a herd I bargained for. We ain't gonna farm. The season's too short, but we'll work our cattle together, and we'll drive to market together. We can use a young buck like you who's not afraid of work. How about coming along?"

"I'm broke," Brad had said. "I wouldn't fit."

Cory had laughed then. "Sure you'll fit. I'll loan you enough to get started. Don't ask me why except that I kind of cotton to you. I'll give you all the time you need to pay me back. It's a chance of a lifetime, I tell you."

"Let me sleep on it," Brad had said.

So he'd slept on it, and he'd dreamed about Jeanie. When he woke, there was Jeanie bending over a campfire, talking with Cory and laughing, a trim, supple girl who had gathered into her slim body and sharp mind everything that Brad Wilder had ever wanted in a woman. Ten minutes later he had told Cory he'd go along.

Now he fired his cigarette and flipped the charred matchstick into the dust. He hadn't told Jeanie he loved her, mostly because he was head over heels in debt to Cory. Perhaps it was false pride. He wasn't sure, but he wanted things to be right when he proposed.

He untied the team, and stepped into the wagon seat, thinking it was a great note for Tom Hildreth to tell him to ask Cory to encourage Nick Bailey. Well, he'd do it because he'd promised Hildreth, but it would be a waste of breath.

"Wilder."

It was young Bailey, standing in the saloon door. Brad said: "Well?"

Bailey came out of the saloon, reeling a little, and grabbed the hitch rail. He said, thick-lipped: "I've got something to say now, Wilder. You stay away from my girl."

"I'll stay away from Jeanie when she tells me to," Brad said. "Not before."

"I'm telling you to!" Bailey shouted. "She's my girl. We're engaged. We're gonna be married. Savvy?"

"You can go to the devil," Brad said, and drove away, leaving Bailey hanging to the hitch rail and cursing him in a blurred drunken voice.

Brad followed the wheel ruts made by Cory Steele and the other settlers who lived south of Getalong. A mile from the store the ruts turned east, keeping to the dry sage flat above the lake that lay to Brad's right, a blue center of a green oasis. Tules crowded the shore, acres of swampland that Cory Steele swore he would drain someday and then he'd have the best grass land in the state, but that day was far ahead. It would take time, and now Brad wondered if there was any.

There were two worlds here, one surrounding the other. The desert lay all around, drab and gray even now in June. The rattle of Brad's wagon stirred a band of antelope into flight away from the road. Young hawks in a nest under a sagebrush clump showed their youthful belligerence as Brad passed, and somewhere off to his left a meadowlark gave out its sweet song.

The other was a water world of lake and swamp, of tules and coon-tails and willows, and grass that by fall would be high enough to hide a calf. Here were the bragging trumpeter swans, pelicans and egrets, herons and ducks and geese. Kildeers rose in front of Brad's wagon and fled, calling out plaintively.

There was a third world, too. It was twenty miles away. That was the high country of the Steens Mountains to the south and the Blue Mountains to the north, summer range for all the cows that the settlers would ever own. The first day Brad had seen this country he had understood why

Cory Steele had brought his people here, why he had told Brad that night that here was their big opportunity.

For the first time since he had come to the valley, Brad was not stirred by this land, and, for the first time, he found himself doubting Cory's judgment. It would be a cruel thing to bring people here, encourage them to build their cabins and make their homes and dream their dreams, and then have everything taken from them. Cory would not knowingly do anything that was cruel. Brad did not question his intentions, but on the other hand he could not help questioning his judgment—if what Whang Dollit was telling was the truth.

Brad passed old Rimrock O'Shay's cabin and waved to him, passed the Widow Bain's place and waved to her. They were typical of the people Cory had brought to the valley. They had believed in Cory Steele just as Brad had believed. To them Blue Lake Valley had become a Promised Land. Anger began to burn in Brad as he thought of this. As Tom Hildreth had said, there seemed to be no reason for Whang Dollit to lie.

In early afternoon, Brad came to the place that was set on a grass-covered bench above the lake. It testified to Cory's wealth just as did the fact that he paid cash to Hildreth for everything he bought. It was the only cabin in the valley that had more than one room. There was one large room across the front that faced the lake. The rear half was divided between the kitchen and Jeanie's bedroom.

Jeanie had seen him coming. She stepped out of the kitchen door and waved to him, her full lips smiling. When he pulled up, she came up to the wagon.

"Get the tomatoes?" she asked.

He sat motionless, his eyes on her. She was something of a tomboy who could ride any horse in the valley; she liked to hunt, and she was a good shot. Because she was honest and inherently good, he wondered if she knew what she had done to Nick Bailey and every single man in the valley, including Brad.

"You know you're as pretty as a new red-wheeled buggy, don't you?" Brad asked.

Stepping back, she put her hands on her slim hips and frowned reprovingly. "You didn't stay in Tom's store like I told you, did you?"

"Why?"

"It would take some of his whisky to put that blarney on your tongue," she said sternly. "Now did you or did you not get the tomatoes?"

"No. Hildreth didn't have any. He says he's got some coming."

"Coming!" she cried. "What good will that do? Dad needs. . . ." She stopped. "Well, that's what we get for depending on Tom Hildreth. I told Dad he ought to send a wagon of his own to The Dalles as soon as the snow went off, but he wouldn't do it."

Brad cuffed back his hat. "Jeanie, did Cory ever make a mistake?"

"He made a mistake when he didn't send a wagon out. . . ." She stopped as if sensing something in Brad's tone she didn't like. "What kind of a fool question is that?"

"It was a fool question, I guess," Brad admitted. "I'll lug your stuff in. Tom had everything but the tomatoes."

He carried the supplies in, and put the team away. He had to see Cory, and it wouldn't be an altogether pleasant talk. For half an hour he cut wood, wondering just what he would say.

Jeanie put her head through the kitchen window. "Your dinner's ready, Brad."

20

He drove the axe into the chopping block and, picking up an armful of wood, carried it into the kitchen. Cory had hobbled in from the front room and sat at the table, smoking his pipe.

"Good trip, Brad?" he asked.

"Fair." Brad poured water into the wash basin from a bucket and washed the dust off and combed his hair. "Dollit and Bailey were at Hildreth's."

Cory took his pipe out of his mouth, dark eyes pinned on Brad. He had been a big man, decisive of motion and speech, but he had thinned down until his cheek bones seemed about to burst through his skin. His face, which had been deeply tanned, had lost its color. But there was a greater change in him than the mark of poor health, and Brad knew that Jeanie worried about it. Two months of idleness had gone hard with Cory Steele, and it galled him to be dependent upon his neighbors, for he was a man who had never depended upon anyone but himself.

Brad sat down and began to eat.

Jeanie asked: "Want a cup of coffee, Dad?"

"No, thanks." Cory had let his pipe go out. He fired it, pulling hard for a moment before he said: "You act like you heard something."

"I did. We've got a swamp angel in the valley."

Cory emitted a sulphurous exclamation, and Brad went on to tell him what Dollit had said, adding: "He asked a good question. Where does that leave us?"

"It don't change nothing," Cory said sharply. "Dollit's lying."

"Why would he lie?"

Cory shrugged his shoulders. "Dunno, but I don't trust Whang Dollit no more than you do. I always did figure he was more than just a man on the dodge. From the first day

21

he hit this valley, he started his talk about how we couldn't last. Now he comes up with this."

"You think there ain't no Riley Rand?"

"That I wouldn't know, but if there is, I'll bet my bottom dollar he ain't bought the valley from the state of Oregon."

Brad finished his stewed prunes. Pushing back his chair, he said: "You've got enough wood to last a few days, Jeanie."

"Thanks," Jeanie said. "I don't know how we could have got along without you. Nick will be out Sunday. He can chop enough to run all week. You can't go on neglecting your own work like this."

Brad had forgotten about young Bailey. He turned to Cory. "Hildreth's worrying about Nick's drinking. He figures you can help him. Give him a job. Invite him out for a meal. Or something."

"I'll do something. I'll break his danged neck. That'll stop his drinking." Cory pulled himself upright and, balancing on his good leg, reached for his crutches that were leaning against the wall. "Come in here, Brad. I've got talk to make."

Cory hobbled into the front room, and dropped down on the leather couch where he spent most of his time. Brad hesitated, thinking of a dozen things he had to do at home.

Then Jeanie gave him a shove, whispering: "Go on, Brad. He's lonesome."

"I get lonesome, too," Brad said.

Jeanie threw back her head and laughed. "If you come over some evening when there's a full moon, I'll take care of that."

"There's a dance Saturday night . . . ," Brad began.

She put a hand on his arm, her face showing genuine regret. "I'm sorry, Brad. I'd be glad to go with you, but Nick's already asked me."

Without another word Brad wheeled from her and stalked into the other room. Cory was filling his pipe, scowling. He motioned for Brad to sit down. Then he asked: "What was the idea of telling me to help Nick?"

"Hildreth asked me to."

"Tom's a fool. I don't figure Nick Bailey is worth saving, and I'm damned sure I don't want him hanging around here. I'll shoot him between the eyes before I'll let him marry Jeanie. He wasn't any good when we lived in the Willamette Valley, and now that he's running around with Dollit, he's worse than no good."

"That what you wanted to say?"

"No. I'm gonna say something else first." He held his pipe in his hand, dark eyes studying Brad a minute. Then he said in a low tone: "I got the notion from a few things you've said that you were going to ask Jeanie to marry you."

Brad rose. "I can't. Not till I get ahead a little."

"Sit down," Cory said. "Maybe I'm talking out of turn, Brad. But if you love Jeanie, you'll ask her to marry you. If you don't, why, just forget everything I've said."

Brad sat down again, and leaned forward. "I've loved Jeanie from the first time I saw her, and I'll go on loving her as long as I live, but everything I've got except my horse and saddle I'm in debt to you for. A man's got to have some pride if he's worth a damn. That's why I've held back. I wanted to get ahead a little."

"And waste the best years of your life because of your pride?" Cory shook his head. "You're wrong, Brad." He shifted his weight, gritting his teeth against the pain. "I ain't fooling myself, boy. This leg ain't getting no better. Maybe I'll never sit a saddle again. I dunno. I know one thing,

23

though. You'd take care of Jeanie if something happens to me, and Bailey wouldn't."

Brad held his silence then, knowing he had said all he could say. He had been through this in his own mind many times. It wasn't entirely his pride that had held him back. Jeanie was nineteen, but Brad felt she would need another year before she would be ready to settle down. And then, too, his own prospects would be better at the end of that year.

"I'm sorry I said all of that," Cory said finally. "Just busted out of me. When it comes to marrying, a man has to decide for himself. What I wanted to talk about was something else."

Cory took his pipe out of his mouth and looked down at it. "Like I said, Brad, I ain't fooling myself. I can't get to a doctor, so I'll keep on being a cripple, or I'll get well according to what old Mother Nature says. Either way, I ain't much use to the folks I brought here. They need someone to do their fighting for 'em. The land we've settled ain't really swampland, and Riley Rand or nobody else is taking our places away from us. We'll fight. . . ."

"Wilder," a man called from outside, "I told you to stay away from my girl!"

Brad rose and checked his gun, giving Cory a thin grin. "Sounds like Nick Bailey. I guess he's a little proddy."

Brad went out through the front door, and circled the house. Nick Bailey was sitting his saddle just beyond the chip pile, his hat cuffed at the back of his head, his thin face dark with the rage that gripped him. Jeanie stood looking up at him. She was talking in a tone so low that Brad could not hear what she was saying.

Brad stopped at the corner of the house. He said evenly: "What's biting you, Nick?"

Jeanie whirled. "Go back and stay with Dad. Nick wanted to see me."

"That's funny. Sounded like he yelled at me."

"No, he doesn't want to see you!" Jeanie cried in a ragged voice. "Go on back."

But Brad stood motionless, meeting Bailey's cold direct stare.

"Whang kept telling me how it was, Wilder," Bailey said. "I should have believed him all the time."

"Just how did Whang say it was?" Brad asked coolly.

"He said you kept coming over here to help Cory out, but all you wanted to do was see Jeanie. He said you was just using Cory's trouble as an excuse."

"It's a good excuse," Brad said. "A lot to be done around here that Jeanie can't do, but I ain't seen you were doing much of it. I've been figuring you were a mite lazy, Nick. Otherwise you could use the same excuse."

"Brad, go back into the house," Jeanie begged. "This won't help any of us."

Brad shook his head. "Nick wanted to see me, Jeanie. I aim to give him so much chance to see me that he'll get a stomach full."

"I got that already!" Bailey shouted. "I'm sick of the sight of you. It's a purty danged poor excuse of a man that'll steal another man's girl. Jeanie and me was engaged when we left the Willamette Valley. Now I ain't sure how I stand with her since you horned in."

"How about it, Jeanie?" Brad asked. "You engaged to Bailey?"

She backed away, biting her lower lip, her face pale. "He never gave me a ring. It was just kind of an understanding." She whirled to face Bailey. "You aren't being fair, talking this way, Nick. You couldn't expect a girl to marry you, the way you've acted since you got here."

"You sound like your dad," Bailey said bitterly. "Before I left Getalong, Whang said I was a fool to let you kick me around like this. He said the only thing to do was to lick hell out of Wilder, and that's what I'm going to do."

Bailey swung out of his saddle, unbuckled his gun, and tossed it on the ground beside the chopping block. Jeanie ran to him and gripped his arms.

"This won't settle anything, Nick. Get back on your horse. I'll see you at the dance Saturday night, and if you. . . ."

"Take off your gun belt, Wilder," Bailey said in a metal-thin voice. "When I get done with you, you won't be in no shape to kiss my girl."

Brad unbuckled his gun belt, and dropped it. Before it touched the ground, Bailey had pushed Jeanie roughly aside and came at Brad in a wild, senseless rush, both arms swinging. Brad stepped aside and threw a right that knocked Bailey flat.

Nick Bailey was a crazy man. He bounced back up, wasting breath in a string of oaths. He was swinging from his knees and making no effort to defend himself, and for the second time Brad let go with a right. Bailey spilled out full-length on the ground and then sat up, shaking his head, blood running down his chin from a cut lip.

"If you've had enough," Brad said, "get on your horse and drift."

Bailey said nothing. He got to his feet more slowly this time and moved in cautiously, his guard up. Brad stepped back, but Bailey caught him by the leg and brought him to the ground.

Brad went down hard, the fall knocking the wind out of him, and Bailey fell on him. They went over, Bailey underneath, and over again, Bailey using his knees and elbows. Brad heaved over, clubbed Bailey on the side of the head, and broke free. He got to his feet and stood there, waiting.

Bailey raised himself on one elbow and stared at Brad, hate in his eyes, blood drooling down his chin. He lay close to the chopping block, and now he rolled over in a sudden swift motion and grabbed for his gun belt. Brad was caught flat-footed, his own gun belt twenty feet behind him, but Brad took the chance of going for his gun, wheeling and lunging toward it. He heard Jeanie scream: "Don't do it, Nick, don't do it!" Then Brad fell flat on his stomach, clawing desperately for his gun and knowing that time had run out for him. But the gun that sounded was not Bailey's .44. It was a rifle cracking from the kitchen door.

"Drop it," Cory yelled. "Drop it, or by gad my next slug is going into your brisket instead of the chopping block."

Brad had his gun clear by then and was scrambling to his feet. Jeanie stood with both hands at her throat.

"I said drop it," Cory repeated. "I ain't saying it another time."

Bailey let go of his gun. He came to his feet, still watching Cory. Without a word he moved past Brad, lurching drunkenly. He reached his horse and stood there a moment, gripping the horn, before he pulled himself into leather.

Brad walked toward him. He said: "I've got nothing against you, Nick. Let's forget it."

"I'll forget it when you're dead," Bailey said thickly.

"Use your noggin," Brad pressed. "Go back to your folks and help 'em out. You haven't done a day's work since you started riding with Whang Dollit. That won't get you any-where, and you know it."

27

"It'll make me a sight more money than chasing after a few cows."

Jeanie came up with his hat and handed it to him. She said in a low, tight voice: "You tried to kill him, Nick. What's got into you?"

Bailey took the hat, and put it on. "I will kill him," he said. He gave Cory a wicked look, then reined around, and rode away.

"You can't make no mistake now, Jeanie!" Cory shouted. "You've got Bailey's size. You got Brad's, too. You. . . ." Then he lost his grip on the doorjamb and fell forward into the yard, face down.

Jeanie screamed and ran to him, Brad a step behind her. She knelt beside her father; she felt of his face, and took one of his thin hands in hers. She began to cry then and, looking up at Brad, asked: "Is he dead?"

"Fainted, I reckon," Brad said. He lifted Cory, carried him through the kitchen to the front room, and laid him on the couch, surprised at how light he was. He felt of Cory's pulse, and stood up. "He's all right, Jeanie. He just hasn't got much strength any more."

She sat down on a chair, her shoulders slack, her face very pale. She whispered: "He was right about Nick, Brad. I've just been bull-headed."

"I was wrong myself," Brad said. "I didn't figure he'd make a try for his gun."

"What's happened to Nick?" she asked.

"I don't know," Brad answered. "I've been wondering what he meant when he said he'd make more money riding with Dollit than he would chasing after cows."

Her hands fisted in her lap, clenched so tightly that her knuckles were white. "I haven't been a very good daughter, Brad. I've wanted my own way. That's all. I haven't liked Nick for a long time."

Turning, Brad left the room, and walked through the kitchen and on to the chip pile. He picked up Bailey's gun and belt, and jammed the .44 into the holster.

Cory was conscious when Brad came back into the house. When he saw Brad, he said: "It's a great thing to be as useless as I am."

Brad laid the gun on the table. "Then I guess I ain't worth much. You just saved my life, you know."

"You know I didn't mean that. Fainting was what I meant, flopping out there like a nervous woman looking at a spoonful of blood."

"I'm gonna find this Riley Rand, if he's in the valley," Brad said. "I've got to see if any cows got bogged down first, then I'll take a sashay south to the rim and see if he's there like Dollit said."

Cory gave him a straight look, his eyes very dark and bright against the pale gray of his face. "What are you thinking, Brad?"

"Maybe what you were thinking a while ago. I reckon I'm just a little slower in the head than you are. Seems kind of funny, Dollit being right about a cowman coming here to the valley and Bailey saying he'd make money riding with Dollit. Looks like they're all playing the same tune."

"Yeah, we're thinking the same thing. I figure there's a hook-up between 'em, all right, but they won't steal our homes, Brad. We'll fight 'em to hell and back."

"Keep a gun handy," Brad said. "Jeanie, you'd best stick pretty close to home."

"Why?" she asked.

"Because Cory's our brains. If he was dead, the settlers would scatter like a band of bleating sheep."

She jumped up, her head back. "Brad, you don't think

Nick came out here to kill Dad? I thought. . . ."

"I don't know," Brad cut in. "I just don't know, but things don't smell good."

"I ain't sure about how smart you are, looking for this Rand *hombre*," Cory said. "Better get a few of the boys together before you start out."

"I'll see," Brad said, and turned to the door.

"Brad," Cory said.

Brad stopped, and swung back. Cory was breathing hard, the corners of his mouth working a little as if he were under a great emotional strain.

"What is it?" Brad asked.

"This will be a fine valley in a few years, if we're let alone," Cory said, "but it's like you say. If I was dead, everybody'd run like sheep." Cory wiped a hand across his forehead and brought it away damp with sweat. "What I'm trying to say is that I feel like my sand's run out. It's gonna be up to you."

"Me?" Brad stared at him, shocked. "Why, I've just been a fiddlefoot as long as I can remember. Nobody can take your place, Cory. I couldn't, anyhow."

Cory smiled. "You could if you believed in something strong enough."

Brad gestured wearily. "Sure, I believe, but. . . ."

"No buts." Cory lifted a thin hand. "Listen to me, boy. Listen close. I gambled on you right from the start, and I wasn't wrong. There isn't another fellow in the valley who can handle a gun like you can. You've got backbone, and you've got integrity. That's the big thing. If you've got that and enough faith, why . . . you can do anything."

"You'd better get some sleep," Brad said. "I think you're out of your head." He dropped the three silver dollars on the table that Hildreth had given him. "There's your change. Almost forgot about it."

He left the room, not looking at Jeanie. He saddled his buckskin that he had left in the corral and, mounting, rode around a shallow corner of the lake toward his cabin. He could not get Cory's words out of his mind. The trouble was Cory didn't know the whole truth. Brad had come along because Jeanie was coming. He had never told either Cory or Jeanie that, but he knew now he would have to tell Jeanie. He could wait no longer.

Brad looked southward to the frowning rimrock, looked at the desert sweep of the land, tilting upward away from the lake, and he wondered what went into the making of a man like Cory Steele, what had given him his great faith, what made people look to him for leadership. Then something tightened inside Brad Wilder and brought an uneasiness to him. Today, without actually putting it into words, Cory had tried to tell him that he had a feeling he would not live to see done the things he had dreamed of doing.

Brad stopped at his cabin long enough to get into his "muddling clothes". He picked up a shovel that leaned against the wall beside the door, and stepped back into the saddle. Just west of his cabin lay a stretch of mud flat that was a deathtrap for cows. Even from here he could see that one was bogged down.

Something had to be done about the mud flat. A fence would have to be built, or the flat drained. There was no wire in the valley, and it was a long way to the Blue Mountains to get poles.

It was well along in the tag end of the afternoon now, with the sun dipping down toward the western rimrock, and a chill wind had come up that stirred the water of the lake into small chopping whitecaps. Brad dismounted and set to work digging the cow out.

By the time the job was done, Brad was cold and tired, his temper was whetted to a fine edge, and he looked like a mud man.

Brad did not see the three riders coming across the grass until one of them raised a hand, calling out: "You Brad Wilder?"

The one who had called would be Riley Rand, Brad judged. Brad said—"I'm Wilder."—and waited, wondering about this. It seemed strange that a newcomer like Rand would know his name. Then he saw that one was a woman, the other a young man in his middle twenties, medium tall and slender.

They pulled up twenty feet away, Rand saying: "Looks like you had a little fun."

"In my book it ain't fun," Brad said shortly, thinking he must be a sight, plastered with drying muck as he was.

"I'm Riley Rand," the man said as if expecting his name to mean something.

He was a big man, this Rand, big and impressive-looking with a square jaw and bold blue eyes that were as frosty as two pieces of ice. He had long muscular arms and big hands, and there was about him the confident air of a man who would push and crowd and shove until anything and everybody who blocked his path had been moved aside.

"I've heard of you," Brad said.

"My sister, Gail."

Rand motioned to the woman who sat her side-saddle with cool grace. She was about twenty-five, Brad guessed, with blue eyes and hair as yellow as ripe bunchgrass. She gave an impression of tallness and had much the same air of complete self-confidence that her brother had. Irritation

32

stirred in Brad as he touched his hat brim. She was giving him a look of sharp appraisal as if wondering just what sort of man was under all the mud.

Rand indicated the man to his left. "Wilder, meet Smoke Kinnear. You've probably heard of him."

Masking his face against the shock of surprise, Brad said: "Howdy, Kinnear. Ain't you off your reservation a little?"

"A little," Kinnear said.

Brad had heard of the man all right. Anyone who had spent some time in the Southwest would have heard of Smoke Kinnear. He carried two .44s, butts forward, the holsters low and tied down in the manner favored by professionals. He had a thin face with a saber-sharp nose and pale blue eyes that were insolently defiant.

Brad had expected Rand to shout loudly that he owned the valley and was giving everybody so many days to clear out. But Rand did nothing of the kind. He fired his cigar, glancing at the few cows grazing to his right.

"How many head of cattle in the valley, Wilder?" he asked then, his tone friendly.

" 'Bout a thousand."

"How many people?"

"Twenty families and a few single men."

Rand scratched his wide chin, looking at the lake and frowning. "They tell me that when this swampland is drained and the tules cleaned out, you have wonderful grass land. Sort of sub-irrigated, I suppose."

"I've heard that," Brad said carefully, wondering what Rand was getting at.

"Just what sort of claim do these settlers have to their land, Wilder?" Rand asked.

"Squatters' rights."

"I see," Rand said. "Kind of risky, ain't it, settling here

33

without knowing they'll ever be able to file on their places?"

"Maybe."

Rand grinned. "Well, we're just taking a ride to see what the valley looks like." He jabbed a forefinger at a cabin a quarter of a mile to the west. "Who lives there?"

"Al Benton and his wife and three kids."

Rand jerked his head at the others. "Let's ride. We'll see you again, Wilder."

They turned their horses westward and rode away. Brad watched them for a minute, still puzzled, and then swung his buckskin toward his cabin. Dollit, he supposed, had told them his name. The talk, to Brad's way of thinking, made less than sense. Rand didn't look much like a schemer. Why hadn't he just come out and said he owned the valley and to get off his land?

Brad put his horse away, and went into the cabin, still wondering about Rand. He was washing up when he heard a horse. It was Rand's sister Gail.

Brad stepped to the door. He said: "Howdy, miss."

She came in, giving him that sharp look of appraisal again. She smiled then. It was as if a shade had been lifted from her face. She seemed very friendly, the calculating sharpness gone from her eyes. "I guess you didn't expect me to come calling." She gave a quick glance around the room that was bare of everything except the sheer necessities for living, and brought her eyes up to him again. "Opening up a new country is a grim life for a while, isn't it?"

"We were getting along," he said, irritation growing in him.

"You need a woman, Mister Wilder. I never could see any reason for a man living alone. But then I hear you have your loop on a girl."

34

"You're heard a lot in the time you've been here," he said hotly. "If you want to give advice, try handing some out to your brother."

Her lips tightened. "I'm sorry, Mister Wilder. I didn't come here to give you advice. Not this kind, and, as for my brother, he doesn't take advice. I've tried." She smiled again, apologetically. "Believe me, I came here for two reasons, both friendly. One was to tell you to watch out for Smoke Kinnear."

"If you think I spook that easy. . . ."

She raised a hand. "Now, Mister Wilder, you're sizing me up wrong. I told you I came for friendly reasons. You strike me as being a man who can take care of himself in almost any situation, but, you see, Kinnear isn't a man. He's a machine, a killing machine."

She was frankly pleading with him now, and the anger went out of him. He said: "All right. I'm warned. I'll watch out for him."

"That's better. You see, my brother and I don't agree on ways and means. The trouble with Riley is that he believes anything is all right, if it works." She hesitated, and then shook her head. "Maybe I'm wasting my time and yours, too, but the real reason I came was to ask you to have supper with us tonight."

It was the most surprising thing she could have said. He hesitated, wondering if this was a trap.

"I'd like to," he said, "but. . . ."

"I know what you're thinking. We're enemies by virtue of our position, but remember, Mister Wilder, that there are several grades of enemies. You said there were twenty families here in the valley. What happens in the next few days will determine whether the women and children of these families are left without husbands and fathers."

35

So that was it! Again anger crowded him. He shouted: "If you think we'll bluff . . . !"

"You can stop right there. Riley is a hard man. He wouldn't have Smoke Kinnear with him if he wasn't. The point is I'm not as willing to shed blood as Riley is. A friendly talk won't hurt, and it might help. Tomorrow will be too late."

Again he had the feeling she was pleading with him. He sensed an earnestness about her that seemed sincere.

"All right. I'll be along as soon as I shave," he said.

"Thank you. Our camp is directly south of here."

Half an hour later Brad was riding south, the sun barely showing above the western rimrock. By the time he reached the Rand camp, the valley lay shrouded under purple dusk. There were two wagons, he saw, and a tent that was possibly Gail's. A Chinese cook was bending over the Dutch ovens as Brad dismounted.

Riley Rand drifted up, saying: "Glad you could come."

"Friendly of your sister to ask me," Brad said.

Rand laughed softly. "It was her idea. We're a lot alike, Gail and me, when it comes to going after what we want, but we're different when it comes to method. Oh, Wilder, meet George McCloud."

Another man had come up, a short, heavy-set young man who was a little too paunchy for his years. He was wearing a brown broadcloth suit and a black derby, and, when he held out his hand, Brad found that it was soft and a little moist.

"Glad to know you, Wilder," McCloud said, his voice definitely that of an Easterner.

"Howdy," Brad said.

Kinnear sat hunkered by the fire, smoking. He ignored

Brad's presence completely. Gail came out of the tent, calling: "Just in time, Mister Wilder! I've been eating like a horse ever since we left Nevada. There's something about your air up here that does things to my appetite."

"Here, here," McCloud said. "He doesn't own the air, you know. That's just taking in too much."

"He doesn't own the land, either, George," Rand said. "We own it. Let's make that clear. Squatters' rights don't hold against a patent."

"No more of that," Gail said sharply. "We'll talk business after supper."

"A good idea," McCloud said heartily. "I don't want my appetite spoiled. That's the trouble with my brother. You've heard of him, Wilder, John McCloud, the railroad man."

"Yes, reckon I have," Brad agreed.

"Well, he's always talking business, morning, noon, and night. That's why I'm here. Had to get away from it. I've got all the money I want. I learned a long time ago that the simple life is the best. This wilderness is paradise. Living in the open, breathing that air Gail was. . . ."

"Let's eat, George," Gail said impatiently. "When you get to talking, you just about starve me to death."

"Oh, I'm sorry, my dear," McCloud said apologetically. "I'm awfully sorry."

But McCloud kept up his talk. Gail was plainly bored, and Brad seemed to be only half listening. Kinnear had taken his plate and tin cup and drifted away.

Time ribboned out into minutes and piled up into half an hour. The last trace of the sunset left the sky. Thunder boomed from somewhere off to the south. Rand tossed some pieces of juniper on the fire and watched the blaze. "I hear a man named Cory Steele is the big gun among the settlers, and he's laid up. That right?" Rand said, his eyes on the fire.

"That's right."

"I also hear that he's got a pile of gold hidden in his cabin. Dangerous, it seems to me, in a country like this."

"Just a rumor," Brad said. "How'd you hear it?"

"Oh, a man picks up things like that," Rand answered.

"Dollit's tale, I suppose," Brad said, and, picking up his plate and cup, carried them to the wreck pan. "Don't believe all his yarns, Rand."

"Dollit?" Rand said as if he couldn't place the name. "Oh, yes, he was the settler who rode in last night to see who we were. Acted like he owned the country."

Brad returned to stand with the fire between him and Rand. Kinnear had drifted back. He stood spread-legged, hands at his sides, his barren face expressionless, pale eyes on Brad. McCloud had moved away toward one of the wagons, and suddenly it struck Brad that Gail was not in sight.

"Might as well get down to cases," Rand said easily. "You've probably guessed why we asked you here. If you've seen Dollit, he may have told you that I have bought this valley from the state, not knowing that any settlers were here. Now I'm faced with a problem. I want them out of the country before my herd gets here."

"Why don't you talk to Cory Steele?" Brad asked.

"Two reasons. He's laid up, so I'm counting him out. Second reason is that I hear he's a fanatic, one of these fellows who won't budge for hell or high water. That's why I'm hoping I can do business with you." He lifted a cigar from his pocket and bit off the end, bold eyes bright in the firelight. "A bunch of settlers always has someone who calls the turn. It's been Steele, but with him on his back it'll be you."

"You're wrong on that," Brad said.

"I don't think so. I can use a man of your caliber in my organization. I pay a good man well, as Smoke can tell you. How about it, Wilder?"

Brad saw it then. He was elected to be an example. He'd be bought, or he'd die. A rage boiled up in him, a cold compelling rage. He had believed Gail Rand and he'd been sucked into a trap. They were alike, Gail and Riley Rand, but because Gail was a woman, she had brought the invitation. The talk about warning him against Smoke Kinnear had been part of the bait, but she had been right about one thing. Kinnear was a killing machine.

Brad was good with a gun, but he stood little chance against Kinnear. Then Brad was remembering some of the things Cory Steele had said, and he knew what Cory would say if he were here. It was a cheap way to clear the valley, a cheap dirty way characteristic of Riley Rand. With Cory laid up and Brad out of the way, there would be no one else to make a stand. Rimrock O'Shay, the Widow Bain, Al Benton, Tom Hildreth. He could name them all. They had followed Cory here, and, without him, they'd go.

So Brad Wilder made his decision. George McCloud and Riley Rand were watching him, waiting. No sound but the crackling of the juniper. A flame leaped up, touching Kinnear's barren face.

"Crawl back under a rock, Rand," Brad said, spacing each word so that it was a slap in Rand's face. "You can go to blazes."

Then Rand moved away, leaving Kinnear and Brad facing each other across the fire.

Chapter Two

For a moment there was no sound but the crackling of the fire and McCloud's heavy breathing. Smoke Kinnear took a sadistic pleasure in watching Brad look at the face of death. But Kinnear didn't draw.

Gail's voice cut across the space between them: "You make a move for your guns, Smoke, and I'll blow your head off."

"Get back into your tent!" Rand bellowed. "Of all the fool things to do. . . ."

"Shut up," Gail said. "You always claim a man can do anything with dollars and guns. If Smoke makes a fast move, I'll show you what a woman can do with buckshot."

"My dear girl . . . ," McCloud began.

"You shut up, too, George!" Gail cried. "I'm running this show till Wilder is out of camp."

"Then I'll be moseying," Brad said. "I wasn't counting on this."

Kinnear gave him a small grin. "Me, neither, Wilder. When Rand hired me, he didn't say he had a hellcat of a sister."

"I didn't know it myself," Rand said.

"Get on your horse, Wilder," Gail said. "I'm apologizing for the Rand style of hospitality. It won't happen again."

"You ain't stopped nothing, miss," Kinnear breathed.

"I don't care about stopping anything. If you and Wilder want to swap lead, it's your business, but it wasn't part of the deal Riley agreed to, and I'll see he keeps his word if I have to convince him with buckshot."

Brad backed toward his horse, and stepped up. "You think maybe I'm a mite faster'n your hired man, Miss Rand?"

"No, but when I invite anyone to eat with us, I don't propose to see him murdered."

"She's right," Rand conceded, "but I hold a pat hand, Wilder. You and your neighbors can sit tight and make me force you off my grass, or you can go peacefully and save trouble for all of us. Which will it be?"

"I ain't speaking for my neighbors," Brad said, "but I will speak for me and Cory Steele. We'll fight you to hell and back. If you ever get our places, you'll have the chore of burying us on 'em. Don't you forget that."

"We could attend to that chore." Rand scratched his head as if puzzled. "I don't savvy you, Wilder. You're too smart to think the Land Office will recognize squatters' rights to land that has been bought from the state."

"That's right," Brad agreed, "but I think you're a liar and a thief."

"Get out of camp, Wilder!" Gail called. "Don't push your luck too far."

Rand's big body stiffened, and his face flamed with fury.

Brad laughed softly. "The truth don't sound good to you, does it, Rand? All right, miss, I'll be glad to ride out of here."

Reining around, Brad headed north, putting his buckskin into a run. When the campfire had become a small red eye in the night, he pulled down to a walk. Sweat broke out

41

on his body as relief rushed through him. He had never wiggled out of a tighter spot than this. He had no illusions about how his gun speed compared with Kinnear's. It had been sheer pride that had made him face Kinnear across the campfire.

Brad was able to smile now that the threat of death had passed. He was thankful to be alive. He was even glad it had happened, for now he understood the Rands. Perhaps he had been foolish to slap Riley with such jarring insults, but it didn't make any difference. He had pledged himself to hang and rattle. His big job would be to persuade the settlers to fight, but he had a feeling that Cory was the only one who could do it.

While he was putting his horse in the corral, it occurred to him he was following Cory's hunch that Rand had not bought the valley. If Cory was wrong, there was no use in fighting. Rand had been right in saying the Land Office would not recognize squatters' rights, if the land had actually been sold. Cory would know that, too, so he must have based his belief on something more solid than a hunch.

Lightning was playing over the sky now, thunder booming steadily overhead. Rain would come soon. Brad barred the door, and went to bed. For a time he lay awake, wondering what Rand's next move would be. Whatever it might be, it would come soon. Then his mind turned to the Easterner. George McCloud seemed entirely out of place with the Rands and Kinnear. He was too soft for this country.

When Brad woke, the sky was cloudless. There was no wind, and the lake was as placid as a great tule-lined mirror. Brad built a fire, then went outside and watered and fed his buckskin. He returned to the cabin and cooked breakfast, watching the valley to the south, for he expected to see Kinnear and Rand ride up.

When he finished eating, he thought of borrowing Cory's team and going after a load of wood. He gave it up at once, for it was a long trip, and this was no time to be gone from the valley.

This was the sort of situation he hated, waiting and worrying and trying to outguess Riley Rand. Brad rolled a smoke, eyes swinging to the south. Nothing was visible except a few cows. He remembered that Al Benton wanted to butcher a shoat. He'd ride over and see if Benton wanted to do the job today. Benton was typical of the settlers, a hard worker who, if let alone, would someday make a home here for his family. While they were butchering, he'd find out if Benton wanted that home enough to fight for it.

Brad saddled his buckskin and stood beside the horse, staring westward. Whang Dollit and Nick Bailey were riding toward him. They had come, he guessed, from Benton's, and he wondered if their visit had anything to do with Rand. He made a quick check of his gun, and eased it back into leather.

"Hey, Wilder!" Dollit called, and motioned to him.

Brad watched the two men ride in. He said—"Howdy, Whang."—keeping his eyes on Bailey as they reined up. Bailey's face showed the marks of Brad's fists but otherwise was a mask of surly indifference.

"We're doing a chore for Riley Rand and ourselves," Dollit said. "Remember what I said about us having a little nuisance value?"

"Yeah, I remember. Are you Rand's chore boy?"

Anger stained Dollit's dark-jowled face. He said sharply: "We ain't hunting trouble, mister, but we ain't against handling it if it bobs up."

"I ain't been hunting it, neither, but it sure as hell has been hunting me."

Dollit laughed as if this was extremely funny. "I heard about that. From the look of Nick's mug, I guess you handled that piece of trouble."

"Shut up," Bailey said. "We ain't here on that account."

Dollit shrugged. "Why, I ain't one to horn into another man's ruckus." He nodded at Brad. "Now just get this notion that I'm running Rand's errands out of your noggin, Wilder. I'm the kind of hairpin who looks out for number one."

"You gonna tell him?" Bailey demanded.

"Yeah. Rand wants to see the settlers in Getalong this afternoon, Wilder. About three. You be there."

"Why?"

"No good reason, maybe," Dollit said smugly, "but was I you, I'd be there. We ain't in no shape to buck Rand, so I say we'd best cash in on our nuisance value if we can."

"I'm bucking him," Brad said flatly.

Dollit grinned as if pleased. "That's your business, friend. I've wanted to see you whittled down ever since I hit the valley. Riley Rand is just the gent who can do it."

"I'm here, and you're here," Brad said. "Why wait for Rand?"

Dollit shook his head. "I'm willing to let Rand do the whittling. I want to get what I can, and then ride out of here. Come on, Nick."

"Wait a minute," Brad said. "Nick, your folks have got a claim. Are they gonna pull out?"

"Dunno," Bailey said, and rode off.

Dollit was in the best humor Brad had ever seen him. Dollit thought, grinning: *They'll pull out all right, but I'm hoping you don't. I'll laugh my head off when Rand nails your*

44

hide to your cabin door. Still grinning, Dollit spurred his horse and caught up with Bailey.

For a long moment Brad stood still, squinting against the bright morning sunlight. This, then, was Rand's move. He'd buy the settlers off if he could. Gail had said he believed a man could so anything with dollars and guns. He'd offer the dollars and threaten with guns, and the chances were good that the combination would work.

Brad remembered Gail had said yesterday that tomorrow would be too late. But tomorrow was today, and it still might not be too late. Paying the settlers something for their rights had probably been Gail's idea. Apparently her brother had thought that with Cory Steele laid up and Brad Wilder dead, guns would do the job without the dollars, but Gail must have had her way.

Mounting, Brad rode eastward, wondering what Cory would say. Rand would not make a big offer. Even if he did, no amount could pay the settlers for the labor and dreams that would be wasted. Brad knew how it was, for he was much like the others. Only Cory Steele and Tom Hildreth had money. The rest had their bare hands, perhaps a team and wagon and a few tools.

A generation before they could have found almost unlimited free and good land. Now most of those places were gone, but the hunger to own their land was as great as it had been with their predecessors. Then, if a man saw a good piece of land he liked, he could claim it and make a home if he had the courage to hold it. That day was gone. It was Blue Lake Valley or nothing, and it would be nothing if Riley Rand had his way.

When Brad came within sight of Cory's place, he saw that Dollit and Bailey had gone on. Quick relief washed through him for he did not want to tangle with Bailey again.

The next time would be final, and he didn't want Jeanie to see it.

Jeanie came out of the house as Brad stepped down and tied. She said nothing until he turned to face her, and he saw that her dark eyes were troubled.

"Dollit and Nick were just here," Jeanie said. "They said there was a meeting with this Rand. What's he up to, Brad?"

"I ain't sure," Brad said. "How's Cory?"

"Poorly. He didn't sleep much last night."

Brad followed her into the house, the slim hope that Cory would be able to go to the meeting dying in him. Cory was stretched out on the leather couch, a pillow under his head. He raised a thin hand in greeting, and his voice was clear and natural when he said: "I had a notion you'd be along, Brad. I didn't get my talking all done yesterday, but I will this morning. Sit down."

"I've got some talking to do myself. Want to hear my yarn first?"

Cory nodded, and began filling his pipe. "Go ahead."

Brad told him what had happened at the Rand camp, Cory smoking without comment. Jeanie stood by the kitchen door, listening.

When Brad finished, Cory said: "Nothing's changed."

"A lot is changed," Brad said irritably. "Rand's got a trail herd coming. If he turns his buckaroos loose on the valley, we're finished."

"Then we'll do the job before his herd gets here," Cory said coolly. "Nothing's changed." He motioned to Jeanie. "Get dinner started."

"It's too early."

"No, it ain't. Brad's going to Getalong, and I figured you'd like to ride in with him."

46

Jeanie disappeared into the kitchen.

Cory knocked out his pipe and motioned Brad closer. "I'm gonna do my talking now. I ain't surprised about Rand's trying to run a sandy on us by claiming he's bought the valley. I've been trying to buy it myself." Cory laughed when he saw Brad's surprise. "I didn't tell anybody but Jeanie. I knew the valley had been declared swampland, but somebody's been blocking me in Salem. Must be Rand. If he gets us out of here, he'll move his herd in. Then all he's got to do is sit tight. Possession is nine points of the law."

"Then you've been playing more'n a hunch."

Cory filled his pipe, struck a match, and sucked the flame into the bowl. "More'n a hunch, but on deals like this you can't be sure. Been a lot of criticism of the way the swampland has been handled. A few men get a big acreage, which same gives the state the sale price of the land, but it don't give many folks a home. That was my ace in the hole. I promised to settle the valley, and I've written to the Land Office telling 'em what I done. For three months I've been looking for a letter saying the deal had gone through, but so far not a word." Cory shifted his weight, biting his lip against the pain that racked his gaunt body. He said: "It's this damned leg that's stopped me. No use trying to go to the meeting. It's up to you."

"I can't. . . ."

"You can, and you will. What happened last night took all the doubts out of my mind." He chewed on his pipe stem a moment, dark eyes studying Brad. "You knew Kinnear could pull faster'n you could. Why did you make a pigeon out of yourself?"

"Pride, I reckon. If I'd caved, I'd never have been able to live with myself again."

"It was more than that, Brad. Maybe you were thinking

47

of Jeanie and the house you want to make for her, but I'm guessing it was mostly because you knew that with me knocked out and you pushing up the clods, Riley Rand would have every settler out of the valley in less than a week."

Brad shrugged. "Have it your way," he muttered.

Cory laughed softly. "I know how it is because there was a time when I was a lot like you. A good hand with a gun but not worth a damn. Just a fiddlefoot looking for a fighting job." Cory drew a deep breath, his face bleak as memories rushed into his mind. "I done a lot of things I ain't proud of. If you're honest, you'll admit you've done a few. That's right, ain't it?"

Brad rose, and walked to the door. "Yeah, that's right."

"I thought so. You or me could have been another Whang Dollit or Smoke Kinnear. You said the Rand woman called him a killing machine. That's a good name. Maybe it's what's down inside a man that makes the difference. Maybe it's other people that changes him. With me it was Jeanie's mother. With you maybe it's Jeanie."

"Maybe," Brad said from the doorway, his back to Cory.

"I'll never forget the first time I saw you," Cory went on, "riding that buckskin like you wasn't going nowhere and didn't give a damn. Toting a gun like you knew how to use it. You know what I thought when I saw you look at Jeanie?"

"No."

"I was seeing myself twenty years earlier. Reckon I had the same kind of a look on my face the first time I seen Jeanie's mother. I said to myself here was a boy I had to take along. Maybe it was crazy, me not knowing anything about you, but I wasn't wrong. I had a feeling about you I can't put into words."

Brad came back to the couch. "Why are you telling me this?"

"Why, I guess I want to prove to myself I was right about you."

"I ain't sloping out if that's what you mean."

Cory shook his head. "It's more'n that, boy. You can't do much alone. If you can hold our bunch together, make 'em turn Rand down no matter how much he offers . . . why, he's licked. As soon as we get news that the land's mine, Rand won't have a leg to stand on."

"I can't talk to 'em," Brad said.

"You'll know what to say when the time comes. Jeanie will be there to side you. Hildreth, too. He's sound. Rand'll be tough, if he can push folks, but I'll bet my bottom dollar he don't want a U.S. marshal in here."

Jeanie came in from the kitchen. "Dinner's ready. Want to come to the table, Dad?"

Cory shook his head. "Fetch it in here."

She went out again.

Cory said: "I told you yesterday I was a leader, but I wasn't when I was your age. I don't know when I learned how to get folks to do what I wanted 'em to, but I did. I ain't even sure why."

Jeanie brought Cory's tray in, and he sat up, pushing the pillow to his back. "Tell 'em that I'll sell their land to 'em and take their notes and give 'em all the time they need."

Jeanie laid the tray on Cory's lap. She said: "We'd better eat."

"I still don't savvy," Brad said.

Cory laughed. "I'll tell you what's the matter. It's the two months I've laid here staring at the ceiling. Nothing to do but think." He waved toward the kitchen. "Go get your

49

dinner, Brad. When you get to town, you ask Hildreth about the mail."

Brad followed Jeanie into the kitchen. She filled the coffee cups, saying softly: "There's something he didn't tell you, Brad. He thinks he's going to die."

"Well," Brad said, "I never heard of a man dying from a broken leg."

He looked across the table at Jeanie, sensed she was thinking the same thing he was. Cory Steele wasn't worrying about dying from a broken leg.

Brad saddled Jeanie's horse while she changed her clothes. He waited in front of the cabin with the horses until she came out, her Stetson dangling down her back from the chin strap. She was wearing a brown riding skirt and a dark blouse; she moved toward him in the quick, graceful way that he had always liked. He gave her a hand up, and for a moment her hand remained in his as she looked down at him.

"Dad has his gun, Brad. He'll be all right." She paused, biting her lower lip. "He will be all right, won't he?"

"Sure," he said, hiding the doubt he felt.

They talked little as they rode north. Brad inwardly resented the job Cory Steele had thrown into his lap but still knew he would do what he could. It was not likely there would be any powder burned today, for Riley Rand would be playing a benevolent rôle, saying he wanted to be fair, that he appreciated the work they had done, and would pay them something for their labor.

Brad tried to think of the right words to make the settlers see that Rand was a thief, wanting to force them off the grass so he could write to Salem and say he was the only one in the valley. His cattle were already grazing here, he'd say, and they'd keep on grazing whether he owned the land or not. The state could take his payment or turn it down.

If the settlers did not take Rand's offer, it would mean war. Rand would leave no doubt in their minds about what would happen. They might have a few days of grace before the herd reached the valley. That would be all. The words Brad needed would come to him. He could only hope that they would come when he needed them, as Cory had said they would.

It was a good day, filled with sunlight, and it struck Brad that there should never be trouble here. This valley had enough water and grass and land for everyone. Time! That was the one thing they didn't have, not with Riley Rand in the valley and with Smoke Kinnear to back any play he made, Kinnear, the killing machine. It boiled down to the age-old decision of fighting or crawling, of dying or living with the shame that comes with crawling. Brad and Cory knew it was better to die than live with that shame, but the others had not yet learned.

A sense of impending failure settled upon Brad. He glanced at Jeanie, wanting to tell her he loved her, to ask her to wait for him until he could give her the home he wanted his wife to have. Time! That was the answer to every problem here in the valley. But there was no time. He had to wait. If he died this day, or the next, or the day after that, it was better for her if she didn't know.

She smiled at him and asked: "What are you thinking about, Brad?"

"Trouble," he said.

Her smile left her lips. "I know. Funny, isn't it, how we go along for a year without having anything go wrong? Then all of a sudden trouble piles up until you can't see over the top."

"Yeah," he said. "Funny."

They were opposite the Widow Bain's place, a tiny cabin too small for her and her five children. She had lost her husband the winter before. If there had been a doctor in the valley, Jim Bain might have been saved, but the closest doctor was on the other side of the Blue Mountains. So Jim's widow was left with the children, and only Tom Hildreth's generosity had kept them alive.

The widow was hitching up her wagon. She called out: "I'll be along, Brad! Don't you let nothing happen till I get there."

"I'll hold the lid on!" he shouted.

"Cory couldn't come?"

"No," Jeanie called. "He isn't well!"

"Too bad. We need him today."

The widow's words burned Brad's mind like a hot iron. *We need him today.*

A few minutes later old Rimrock O'Shay fell in with them, riding a plow horse that was so slow Brad and Jeanie had to pull their animals down to a snail's pace.

O'Shay asked: "What's this all about?"

"Didn't Dollit tell you?" Brad asked.

"He said something about a cattleman claiming the valley, but, hell, Cory wouldn't have fetched us here unless the land was open for filing. I kept telling him we oughta hike out for Lakeview and file, but he said we didn't have time. Then he got laid up and couldn't go."

"A paper claim wouldn't make no difference to a man like Riley Rand," Brad said. "The homestead law never has meant anything to cattlemen. There's only one thing that does."

"You're talking about fighting," O'Shay said bitterly. "Well, you'll fight alone, Wilder. I've got a wife and a cabin full of kids." His faded eyes were bleak as they stared across the valley. "Sure too bad a man's foresight ain't as good as his hindsight. If I'd knowed Cory was gonna get bucked off a horse and laid up at a time like this, I'd have stayed in the Willamette Valley."

They'll all think the same way, Brad thought. Cory could talk to them, make them believe that fighting and dying was better than crawling and living. A sense of impending failure shadowed Brad's thoughts. If Cory Steele were on his feet—but he wasn't, and no amount of wishful thinking could change that one hard fact.

They rode into Getalong a few minutes before three. The settlers were here, Brad saw at once, all but the Widow Bain, and she'd be along. Several groups were scattered between Hildreth's store and his house; talk rose, a low, worried hum. Dollit and Nick Bailey were standing in front of the saloon with Bailey's father. Dollit's voice rose above the hum: "You boys can do as you damn' please, but me, I'm taking what I can get."

Brad dismounted and gave a hand to Jeanie. Several people crowded around them, asking: "How's Cory?" Jeanie's answer was always the same: "He's poorly. He said he wished he could be here, but he couldn't."

Brad tied his and Jeanie's horses. Old man Bailey drifted up, asking: "What was the trouble between you and Nick?"

"Didn't Nick tell you?"

"No. He said you beat hell out of him."

Brad told him what had happened, watching the old man's bitter eyes darken with anger, and he added: "Nick would have blowed my head off if Cory hadn't horned in. You ain't got much cause to be proud of him since he started traveling with Dollit."

"No," Bailey said somberly. "We should have stayed in

53

the Willamette Valley. We was making a living there. Not much, but a living." He spread his work-gnarled hands in a gesture of hopeless resignation. "Nick's got a place beside mine, you know, but he don't work it. Now he's saying he'll take anything this Rand fellow will give him."

"What about you?"

Bailey stared past Brad at the long dark crest of the Blue Mountains. "I reckon I'll quit, too. Nick's got some good in him, if I can get him away from Dollit. Maybe he'll go back to the Willamette Valley with me."

Brad walked away, not wanting to hurt the old man, but it would take a father, he thought, to see any good in Nick Bailey. Hildreth was in the store talking to Rand and Kinnear. Gail was not in sight. Hildreth stopped when he saw Brad come in. Rand and Kinnear turned, and for a moment Brad faced them, wondering if this was the time, but Kinnear's stony face told him nothing, and Rand hid his feelings behind a mask of friendliness.

"Howdy, neighbor," Rand said. "Still gonna hang tight?"

"You're damned right I am." Brad nodded at Hildreth. "Mail get in, Tom?"

"No, it ain't," Hildreth answered. "Three days overdue. I could understand if it was bad weather, but nothin's happened to hold him up. I can't figure it out."

"Expecting something?" Rand asked.

"Cory was," Brad said, turning away.

A moment later Hildreth left the store, Kinnear and Rand behind him. Hildreth called: "All right, folks. It's three o'clock. Time to start." He climbed the creaking stairs, Rand and Kinnear following. The others hesitated, then formed a line and moved up behind them.

Brad waited for Jeanie who was with the Widow Bain.

They fell in behind the rest, and, when Brad was halfway up, he looked down and saw that Gail and Mrs. Hildreth had just left the house. That was something else to wonder about. Gail had her place in this thing, and it occurred to Brad that she was more to be feared than her brother Riley. Women seldom understood what it meant to a man to fight. Mrs. Hildreth was a tall pale woman who had hated this country from the first.

A table had been placed at the far end of the hall. Rand sat behind it, pen, ink, and paper in front of him. Kinnear lounged against the wall behind Rand, silent and watchful. Half a dozen benches had been arranged in front of the table. Most of the settlers sat down, but Brad remained standing behind Jeanie who sat beside the widow on the rear bench. Looking at the settlers' slumped shoulders, it seemed to Brad that they were beaten before Riley Rand opened his mouth.

Hildreth had been leaning over the table, talking to Rand. Now he turned ponderously, facing the crowd gravely. He said: "Folks, this is a sad occasion. We've come a long ways to find a home, but looks like we picked the wrong spot." He sucked in a wheezing breath. "If Cory Steele was here, he'd be standing before you, but he's doing too poorly to be here, so I'm taking over long enough to introduce Riley Rand to you. I'll let him make his own spiel."

Rand rose as Hildreth sat down. Rand unfolded a map and held it up. "This is a sad occasion for me, too. As you can see on this official map, Blue Lake Valley has been declared swampland by the federal government and turned over to the state of Oregon. It was not open for settlement when you came here a year ago, and it isn't open now." Rand laid the map on the table. "Since Cory Steele is not here, I can't ask him the question that is in my mind and must be in yours. Why did he fetch you here and tell you to settle on land he must have known could not be filed on? Now whether he had some purpose of his own, or just didn't look into the situation, I don't know. Either way, it's rough on you and me, too."

Fury rose in Brad. This was something he should have expected. Riley Rand was coolly setting out to break the settlers' trust in Cory at a time when he wasn't here to defend himself. Brad started around the bench, plenty of words in his mind now, but Jeanie caught him by his arm.

"Wait, Brad," she whispered. "Let's give him all the rope he needs."

He hesitated, looking down at the girl's anxious face and thinking that Cory had foreseen this. He'd probably told Jeanie what to do. Brad nodded, and stepped back behind her.

"Now I'll tell you what I meant by saying this was rough on both of us," Rand went on in a voice that was both worried and friendly. "I have nothing against you folks. You trusted the wrong man, so the mistake wasn't yours. On the other hand, I bought this valley from the state, not knowing it had been settled. I came on ahead of my herd to see how the grass was and found you folks already here and your cattle eating my grass."

"How come you could buy the valley when any fool can see that not much more'n a tenth of it is swampland?" Rimrock O'Shay demanded.

"I hadn't seen the land," Rand answered easily. "I bought it by looking at a map, and the map says it's swampland. Well, it's all right. When I reclaim the swamp, as I have to do according to the terms of the sale, I'll have good hay land. I don't mind saying, folks, that the valley suits me. In another ten years, you'll see the finest cattle ranch in

Oregon right here in Blue Lake Valley."

"I mean how could the state sell land that ain't swamp?" O'Shay persisted.

"The answer to that, my friend, is simple. The state needs money. Nobody in Salem cares whether it's swamp or sage flat as long as the government turns it over and someone has money to pay for it."

Rand paused, bold blue eyes sweeping the room, big hands, palms down, on the table. Even Brad found it hard to believe he was lying, for Riley Rand had the air of a man who could not be doubted and could not be stopped.

"So you see, folks, you have no legal claim to your homes," Rand resumed. "I could give you twenty-four hours to get out of the valley, but that wouldn't be fair. You do have a sort of moral claim, and, as I said, the mistake was not yours. So I'm willing to pay you for your improvements, providing you'll sign over whatever rights you think you have. Actually you don't have any because no Land Office will recognize squatters' rights in the face of a sale like this, but I want to get something for my money." Stooping, Rand lifted several small sacks to the top of the table, the soft *clink* of gold coming to Brad through the oppressive silence. "I told you I wanted to be fair," Rand assured them. "I'll give you five hundred dollars apiece for your places. You're to be out of the valley by the end of the week. That's five days."

"Well, I'll be damned," Dollit said in a pleased voice. "Five hundred dollars! Hear that, Nick? Easiest money a man ever made. Mister, uncork your ink bottle and count out my money."

Dollit swaggered up the aisle, Nick Bailey behind him. Brad sensed a real difference in the two men. Dollit had undoubtedly been playing Rand's game from the first, but

Nick Bailey belonged with the settlers. Whereas Dollit had an assured manner, Bailey had the furtive air of a man who was thoroughly ashamed.

"This is a simple form, Dollit." Rand pushed a sheet of paper across the desk. "Just says you're signing over any rights you have to the quarter section you've been claiming."

Dollit wrote his name and pocketed the gold Rand handed him. Bailey picked up the pen and signed.

Turning her head, Jeanie nodded at Brad. "Time to start the ball."

Brad moved toward the front of the room, calling: "Nick, I didn't figure when the chips were down that you'd sell your saddle like this!"

Bailey grabbed the money Rand was holding out, wheeled, and ran toward the door.

"Wait for me, Nick!" Dollit shouted. "You ain't got nothing to be ashamed of." He walked out with what dignity he possessed.

Rand glared at Brad, his eyes wicked. He said: "Wilder, I aim to keep this peaceable if I can. You can kick hell loose some other time, but right now these folks have a right to get what they can."

"Well, now," Brad said, "I'd just as soon kick hell loose right here as any place. You overlooked one question I aim to have answered. Why haven't you showed us real proof that you own the valley?"

Rand's lips tightened. He nodded at Kinnear, breathing: "He wants proof, Smoke. Show him some."

Kinnear stepped away from the desk so that he faced Brad, the characteristic small smile on his lips. "I've got the proof, Wilder," he said as he patted his gun butts. "Two of 'em."

For a moment there was absolute silence. To Brad, this was the campfire scene all over again. Brad looked into Kinnear's pale, insolent eyes, waiting to see if Kinnear meant business. Again it was Gail who broke it up.

"Riley, pull off your gun dog. I told you to leave him in camp." She jumped up and ran to the front of the room. "Folks, I'm Riley's sister and his partner. I don't want any bloodshed on my conscience. That's why I insisted he make this offer."

"All right, Smoke," Rand murmured. "Let it go."

Kinnear shrugged. "That's twice she's saved your hide, bucko."

Brad wheeled to face the settlers. "It sure gravels me to hear Rand call Cory a liar and hint he was trying to fill his own pockets. You know Cory too well to believe that."

Hildreth rose. "I feel the same way, Brad, but it strikes me that Cory made a mistake. If this comes to a shooting war, I don't want no part of it. One life ain't worth all the damned swampland in the valley."

"Cory would like to hear you say that," Brad breathed. "He told me this morning that you were sound, but, if I'm hearing right, he sure as hell was wrong."

"We ain't fighting men," Hildreth said hoarsely, fat cheeks growing red. He motioned to Rand and Kinnear. "They are. I say we'd better make the best deal we can."

"Maybe you want the *dinero* we owe you," Brad said. "Five hundred dollars apiece would give us enough to pay our store bill."

The color in Hildreth's cheeks deepened. "No, I ain't thinking of that. I just don't want to see good men die for nothing."

"As far as you're concerned, Mister Hildreth," Rand said smoothly, "I won't insist on your leaving the valley. I'll need a store here, so I'll be glad to rent you the land your buildings are on."

It was a smart move, Brad thought. With Cory absent, Hildreth was as near a leader as the settlers had. Rand was counting on him swinging them over. Brad had a hunch that the whole thing had been planned. Kinnear had never intended to pull his gun. It had simply been a gesture to show the settlers what they would be up against if it came to a fight.

But Hildreth did not take the bait. He said: "Thank you kindly, Mister Rand, but I'll go with my friends." Hildreth started toward the table.

Brad said: "Wait, Tom. I've got one more thing to say. I didn't know till this morning that Cory knew the valley had been marked as swampland. He thought he could buy it himself, and he still thinks he'll get it. When he does, he'll sell the land to you folks and give you all the time you need to pay."

"I tell you I've already bought the valley," Rand said hotly.

Brad still faced the settlers. He saw doubt in their faces, for the trust they had in Cory Steele could not be easily killed. He said: "Cory expects to hear from Salem any day. We all know there's been some kick about the way the sale of swampland has been handled. Cory promised to settle the valley. That's why he fetched you here. If we hang tight, we'll win."

"Take my offer or leave it," Rand said ominously.

"We'll leave it!" Brad shouted. "I'm trying to say what Cory would say if he was here. Wait a few days. We don't have to sign anything today. If Rand wasn't worried, he wouldn't be trying to stampede us. Let him fetch a U.S. marshal in here to run us out if it comes to that."

60

Jeanie was on her feet now, her chin thrust forward defiantly. She said: "If Dad was here, that's exactly what he'd say. We can't lose anything by waiting, but we can lose all we've got by signing today."

"Looks to me like Dollit and young Bailey are the only smart men in the crowd!" Rand bellowed. "You'll lose five hundred dollars apiece if you don't sign today. I ain't gonna hold that offer open."

"I'm asking you," Brad flung at them, "whether Riley Rand looks like the kind of man who'd throw ten thousand dollars away unless he figured he didn't have a real claim to the valley?"

Brad saw he had won. They were talking among themselves, and Rand's threatening words—"Come on. I ain't wasting all day here. Line up and get your money."—had no effect on them.

The Widow Bain was on her feet. "I ain't signing nothing, mister," she said, and walked out.

"Me, neither!" Rimrock O'Shay shouted. "Not today I ain't."

Others rose and followed, not even glancing back at the furious Rand. Nick Bailey's folks went with the others. Only Hildreth waited, unhappy and tormented.

Brad said: "I thought you were one man who'd back me."

"All right, Wilder," Rand said in a low wicked tone. "What you done today just made some widows and orphans. I'll clear this valley before my herd gets here. That's a promise."

Hildreth motioned to Brad with a trembling hand. "You made a mistake today, Brad, a bad one."

Without a word, Brad turned to Jeanie who was waiting for him. They went down the stairs together, the warm glow of triumph in Brad. He was thinking of things Cory had said. Cory had said it was Jeanie's mother who had changed him. Well, it was Jeanie who had changed Brad Wilder. Cory had been right about something else, too. There was no sense in throwing away the best years of his life. He'd ask Jeanie, and he'd marry her tomorrow if she'd have him.

Brad did not see Gail until he reached the ground. She said: "Well, Wilder, you pulled it off."

Jeanie faced Gail, coolly appraising her, and it struck Brad that he had never seen two women who were more different. There was nothing girlish about Jeanie now as she stared contemptuously at Gail Rand.

"I'm proud of him," Jeanie said. "I would have been proud of my father if he had been here and said the things Brad said. I never really understood before the things my father likes to say, but I do now."

"What, for instance?"

"That it is better to die for what you believe in than to live and know you're a coward."

Gail was amused. "Tell me one thing, Miss Steele. Have you ever seen a man brought in across his saddle, shot during a range war?"

"No."

"I didn't think so. I have. It's something you'll remember all your life. Don't let it happen here."

"Then you stop it!" Jeanie cried. "I won't."

"You're young and foolish. Brad Wilder will die, and you'll never forgive yourself for the part you had in killing him." She looked at Brad. "You know how it will go, Wilder. You can stop it."

"I reckon not, miss."

"*You* stop it!" Jeanie cried again.

"I can't," Gail said. "I've done all I can. My brother

never lets anyone stop him when he sees something he wants."

"Come on, Jeanie," Brad said. "Let's drift."

Brad and Jeanie walked toward their horses. Gail stood motionless, genuine concern in her eyes. Brad and Jeanie mounted, and rode away. Gail, Brad thought, had been sincere. He had suspected her of playing a part in her brother's scheming, but now he wasn't sure.

Brad had thought in that one fine moment when he'd left the hall and been filled with the bright glow of triumph that he would tell Jeanie he loved her, but the right words would not come, and they rode back in utter silence, Jeanie's face somber and clouded by worry.

They reached the Steele place in early evening with purple shadow clinging to the western rim, the last of the day's sunlight bright upon the eastern half of the valley. Jeanie said: "Stay for supper, Brad. Dad will want to hear all about it."

"Glad to. I reckon Cory will be happy about the way it turned out."

"Yes, he will," Jeanie said, and went into the house.

Brad led the horses toward the log trough, but before he reached it, he heard Jeanie's scream, shrill and terrible with horror. He dropped the reins and ran into the cabin. Jeanie was standing just inside the doorway, her eyes on her father. He lay in the middle of the room, sightless eyes staring upward, his gun a foot from an outstretched hand.

Stooping, Brad felt of Cory's wrist. There was no flicker of a pulse. He had died just as he had expected to. There was a bullet hole in his chest.

Chapter Three

Brad did not know how long he stood there, staring at Cory Steele's body, nor did he know how Jeanie got into his arms, but she was there, crying, and Brad held her as he might have held a child, comforting her. But at this moment for Brad Wilder, it was as if the sun had suddenly refused to shine, and the darkness was all around. In a way Cory Steele had been like an older brother to Brad. He had said frankly he was a leader, but he had not bragged about it. It had been a simple statement of truth. Now he was dead, and those who followed had no one to look to.

Cory Steele had not been at the meeting in person, but it had been his spirit that had beaten Riley Rand. Rand must have sensed the strength that was in Cory even though he was an invalid held within the walls of his cabin. So he had ordered Cory's murder, thinking it would take the heart out of the settlers' resistance.

Without a word Brad led Jeanie into the thinning sunlight. He said: "You can't stay here. We'll go back to Hildreth's."

She gripped his arm. "Brad, who did it?"

He knew, but he looked away from her. "Who do you think?"

"Everyone stayed till the end of the meeting except Nick

64

Bailey and Whang Dollit," she said tonelessly.

Brad shook his head. He did not answer.

"Then it *was* Nick."

"Or Dollit."

She looked westward across the valley where the sun was showing a red arc above the rimrock. "He knew this was coming, and I was impatient with him. I thought he was just tired of being laid up, but he knew, Brad. He *knew*."

It was dark by the time they started back to Getalong, Cory's body wrapped in canvas in the back of the wagon. The cabin had been ransacked, and Cory's saddle horse had been stolen. Brad had made a careful search around the house and barn, but he had been unable to pick up a clue that would identify the murderer. There was no doubt in his mind about it, and he was sure that everyone except Nick Bailey's parents would reach the same conclusion.

"They'll come back and burn our place, won't they?" Jeanie asked suddenly. "It's all part of Rand's scheme to clear the valley, isn't it?"

It was likely, Brad thought, that they would do exactly that.

"They wanted it to look like robbery, didn't they?" Jeanie asked.

"I guess so."

They rode in silence, then, the darkness pressing around them. A light showed in the window of the Widow Bain's cabin. Later they could see Rimrock O'Shay's light, a tiny pin prick in a vast sea of black space.

Once Brad heard Jeanie sob, but he thought it was better to leave her alone. There was nothing anybody could say, now, that would help. Death was not a new thing to him.

Brad wondered what would happen next. The settlers

had defied Rand because they had expected Cory to get back on his feet; they had believed what Brad had said about Cory's buying the valley and selling their land to them. Now, he thought, they would drift away, and that was exactly what Rand expected.

Finally they pulled up in front of Hildreth's house. The door swung open, and yellow light fell through the opening in a long finger. Hildreth called in worried tones: "Who is it?"

"Brad. Jeanie's here, too."

"What brings you back?"

Brad stepped down from the wagon seat as Hildreth moved ponderously across the yard to them. Brad lifted Jeanie down as Hildreth came up, peering questioningly at them in the darkness.

"Cory was murdered this afternoon," Brad said.

Hildreth stopped dead. Mrs. Hildreth had come out of the house in time to hear what Brad said. She began to shriek, a strange, incoherent, unnerving sound.

Hildreth wheeled on her. "Liza, I've never struck you, but, if you don't stop that, I will."

She covered her face with her apron and ran into the house.

Brad said: "I thought you could take Jeanie in. She can't stay there."

"Of course. Come in, Jeanie. I'll get a lantern."

Hildreth walked to the house. Jeanie hesitated a moment, her hand gripping Brad's arm. "Don't let them kill you, Brad," she whispered. "We need you. You know what Dad expected of you."

It was something he had been thinking about all the way in. He had thought that it was a job he could not do. Now he knew he had to do that job. Just how, he did not know.

"My hide's bullet-proof. I wish there was something I could say."

"I know, Brad. There's nothing. He's gone. That's all. You're all I've got now, and I couldn't bear losing you, too, but I know what has to be done."

Turning, she walked quickly into the house, her head high. He watched her disappear inside. She had said: *You're all I've got now.* He knew then that she loved him and wondered why he had not known it all the time. Still, loving him, she had not said: *Let's ride away. You may be killed if we stay.*

Hildreth came out of the house, a lighted lantern in his hand. He said hoarsely: "Drive around to the back of the store."

Brad stepped into the seat, Hildreth following, and Brad drove past the store building and swung in behind it. Hildreth got down and opened the door. He hung the lantern on a nail, and turned back.

"We'll leave him here," Hildreth said. "I'll sit up with him tonight. Looks like we'll be busy for a few days, so we'd best bury him tomorrow. I'll make the coffin in the morning while you're getting word to everybody."

They carried the body inside.

Hildreth wiped a sleeve across his eyes. He said: "It's queer, the way you get to feeling about somebody. Seemed like Cory was immortal. I never thought of his dying."

"What will folks do now?" Brad mused. "Folks counted a heap on Cory. Now he's gone."

Hildreth lowered his gaze. "Rand figured wrong on this. So have you. Cory is going to be bigger dead than he was alive. We won't run, Brad." Hildreth swallowed. "Cut any sign on the killing sons-of-bitches that done it?"

"No."

"Well, don't make no difference. Dollit and Nick Bailey will have a bad time explaining where they went after they left here."

"I don't figure we'll ever see 'em again."

"We'll see 'em, all right. Rand needs their guns. Dollit's, anyhow." Hildreth scratched his bald head. "I can't believe Nick had a hand in it. He ain't much good, but he ain't a killer."

Brad said nothing, but he did not share Hildreth's faith in young Bailey. "Got another lantern?" he asked. "I'll put the horses away."

"There's one hanging just inside the barn door."

Brad's horse had been tied behind the wagon. He untied him now and unhooked the team. He put them and Jeanie's saddle horse away, and returned to the store. He said: "I'll stop at Rimrock's place and send him in. He can spell you off so you can get a little sleep."

"Where are you goin' to stay?"

"Cory's place. Jeanie's afraid they'll burn the cabin."

Hildreth gripped Brad's arm. "You can't do that. Rand's next move will be to get you. Then where'll we be?"

Brad looked at Hildreth's bearded face. Indirectly Hildreth had said the same thing Cory had said a few hours before. *It's up to you.* For the first time in his life Brad felt the weight that Cory Steele had carried for years, the faith and trust of other men. Silently Brad mounted and rode away, leaving Hildreth standing under the lantern and staring anxiously after him.

It took Brad all the next morning to circle the lake and tell the settlers about Cory's death and the funeral. With one exception they received the news the same way. They were shocked. The Baileys were the only ones who varied the pattern. Old man Bailey stood in front of his cabin, the wind riffling his long white hair. His wife was behind him, a tight-lipped little woman with faded sad eyes. Brad felt pity for them. Nick, he had heard, was their only child.

"Who done it?" Bailey asked.

He was the first to ask that question, and Brad found himself looking away toward the wind-tossed surface of the lake. He said: "I don't know."

"But you think you know," Bailey said, "and I think I know. I ain't seen Nick since the meeting yesterday. Now I'll tell you something. If you bring Nick and Dollit in, I'll help hang them both."

Mrs. Bailey cried out and gripped his arm. "No, Paul, no!"

But the old man nodded, the agony of shame in him. "For years he's brought us nothing but trouble. There's only one way to deal with a man when he joins a wolf pack. We'll treat him that way whether he's my son or not."

"Maybe it won't come to that," Brad said, and rode away.

The settlers had begun to gather in Getalong by the time Brad completed the circle. He ate dinner in Hildreth's kitchen, Mrs. Hildreth waiting on him in her silent, distant way, her eyes disapproving when they settled on his gun. Brad did not see Jeanie, but he could hear the hum of low, mournful talk that flowed in from the parlor.

Brad rose when he finished eating, shaking his head at Mrs. Hildreth's offer of more coffee. She came toward him then, her thin face very pale. She said: "They're all talking about you now, Mister Wilder. Because you carry a gun, they think you'll take Cory Steele's place."

"I reckon you're wrong, ma'am," Brad said quietly.

"Nobody can take Cory's place."

"They're talking about revenge," she breathed. "About hanging Dollit and young Bailey and maybe this Riley Rand, but that means fighting. Our men will be killed. Will it bring Cory Steele back?"

He looked at her, wondering if she had been responsible for Hildreth's attitude during the meeting. Brad could not argue with her. He had seen this happen many times before, the women crying for peace and never considering the price of that peace. "You've been listening to Gail Rand," Brad said. "We have to do what we have to do." He pulled away from her grip and left the room.

The grave was not quite finished, and Brad took a shovel and spelled Rimrock O'Shay. By the time it was done, the coffin had been built and lined with black cloth from the store. More wagons were coming in. Before two o'clock every settler in the valley was in Getalong for the second successive day.

The women gravitated toward the house, the men to the rear of the store. They made a solid knot in front of Brad, their eyes expectant. Hildreth said: "It's a little while before we start the service. We'd best decide what to do."

O'Shay threw a hand out toward Brad. "You knew Cory better'n any of us, I reckon. What would he tell us to do?"

Brad hesitated. If any of them died, it would be his responsibility, and the women would hate him as long as they lived. Tight-lipped, Brad said: "You're handing me quite a chore."

"We know that," Hildreth said, "but you're the only one who can handle it. I'm thanking you for keeping me from doing something yesterday that I'd have been ashamed of all my life. I honestly thought Rand owned the valley. If he did, our fighting would be wasted."

"You still don't know Rand wasn't telling the truth."

Hildreth spread his fat hands. "We know all right. If he'd been telling the truth, he wouldn't have had Cory killed."

The rest nodded, and Brad understood what Hildreth had meant the night before when he'd said that Cory would be bigger dead than he had been alive. "There's only one thing to do that I can see," Brad said thoughtfully. "It means some fighting. Maybe some of you will be lying here beside Cory before the week's over."

"We know that," Rimrock O'Shay said with some heat. "I was talking crazy yesterday when I said I didn't want no fighting on account of I've got a wife and kids." He looked past Brad at the open grave. "If Riley Rand gets the valley, there'll be a lot of graves yonder."

There was a murmur of agreement. Even old man Bailey, standing far back in the crowd, showed he'd go along. Brad knew then they would do what Cory wanted. They'd hang and rattle. "All right," Brad said. "Here's what we'll do. Rand said he'd give us five days, but I doubt that he will. He'll be mighty sore because we didn't take his proposition yesterday, so I'm guessing he'll do something like dry-gulching us or burning our cabins. Maybe run our cattle out of the valley."

"Well, then," O'Shay said, "we'd better hit him first."

"That's my idea," Brad said. "Soon as the funeral's over we'll go after Dollit. If we find him, we'll give him a trial and hang him. Then we'll shove Rand and his wagons through the notch and tell him to stay out of the valley. We'll put men around the rim and fix some piles of brush for signal fires. If Rand comes back, we'll kill him. While we're gone, you'd better leave your wives and kids here."

"Say," Al Benton said sourly, "if we do that, they'll burn

71

every cabin in the valley while we're lookin' for 'em."

"There's a chance they might do that," Brad agreed, "but we've got to count on losing something. I'll tell you another thing, Al. Rand claims he's got a herd on the trail. He's probably got ten men, maybe more, with his cattle. If he sends for his bunch, we'll have a fight. But they can't handle us if we get the jump on 'em. We'll wait till dark. Rand won't expect us to hit him."

"Soon as the funeral's over," O'Shay said, "we'll head for home and do our chores, then strike south."

"I'll get a small fire going in the pocket," Brad said. "That's close to Rand's camp, but they can't see us. We'll gather there."

Hildreth glanced at his watch. "Time for the service."

It was a simple service. There was no preacher in the valley, and no time to send to Canon City for one, so Hildreth read from the Bible and prayed.

In the little cemetery later, Jeanie stood very straight with the Widow Bain's arm around her, as the coffin was slowly lowered into the grave. Then the widow led her away, and Brad picked up a shovel and helped fill the grave.

They broke up then. Brad saw that most of the wagons were leaving without the women and children. Brad saddled and rode around the store, and, when he passed the house, he saw Jeanie on the porch. She waved, and walked down the path to him. He reined up, wondering what he could say to her.

Jeanie smiled when she came up, a small curve of her lips. She said: "Brad, there was a lot about Dad's past he never told anyone but me. But all the time since I can remember, he's been a good man. I didn't sleep any last night. Maybe I imagined this, but it seemed to me he was in the room, talking to me. That's why I didn't cry today. The grief I feel is for myself. I think Dad is very happy."

He saw that there was no real sadness in her face, and it surprised him. He had been wrong in thinking tears would help. Not Jeanie Steele. There was nothing girlish about her now. These last few days had matured her.

"Don't go back to your place," Brad said.

"I won't," she promised. "Not till this is over. Take care of yourself, Brad."

"I figure on doing that," he said, and rode away.

The sun had dipped toward the west, its sharp glare upon the valley, but the wind was still bitter. *A good day for Cory's funeral,* Brad thought. Then he lowered his gaze to the wheel ruts that ran ahead of him, and the weight of reality became a load upon him.

Brad was the first to reach the pocket, a shallow cave in the rock wall a mile east of the Rand camp. He was out of the wind here, but it was still cold. He built a fire and held his hands out to it, and grew impatient with the waiting, but there was nothing to do for a time.

They began drifting in presently, Rimrock O'Shay and Al Benton and some others, riding singly and making a wide swing across the sage flat. If Rand had run into any of them, they could have said they were out looking for cattle, but neither Rand nor Kinnear had been seen. The Rand campfire, O'Shay reported, looked like a house burning down. It was that big.

Uneasiness touched Brad. A fire that big was wasteful, and Rand, Brad judged, was not a man who would be wasteful of anything without a purpose. Perhaps the fire marked an empty camp, intended to lull the settlers into a sense of security. There was something else, too, that surprised Brad and added to his uneasiness. Anger had grown in these men since the funeral until now it was a cold re-vengeful rage. Their talk was wild, and impatience prodded them. They wanted to hang everybody they caught, in-cluding Gail Rand.

"It ain't good enough just to run them Rands out of the valley," O'Shay cried. "They'll come back with their tough hands and wipe us out."

"Maybe, but hanging a man is mighty permanent," Brad said quietly. "Cory believed in a lot of things that were good for the valley. One was law. He said we had to avoid anything that would give us a bad name."

"Bad name!" O'Shay bellowed. "We'll have a bad name if we let this go!"

"We won't let it go," Brad said. "I told you we'd try Dollit, if we find him. Nick Bailey, too. If they killed Cory, we'll hang 'em, but we've got no hanging charge against the rest."

O'Shay's eyes dropped under the pressure of Brad's stare, but he remained sullen and unconvinced. A few hours before, O'Shay and the others had been meek enough, un-certain whether to fight or run, but now they were filled with a lust to kill that only Cory Steele's murder could have aroused in them.

There were fifteen men standing around a fire. Studying them, Brad saw the same sullen rage on every weather-burned face from Rimrock O'Shay's grizzled one to that of Al Benton who was the mildest man in the valley.

"Hildreth said he'd stay till dusk in case the mail got in," Brad said. "We'll have to wait for him, but I think I'll take a sashay over to Rand's camp just to see how the land lies. You boys stay here."

They nodded, saying nothing, but Brad wasn't sure they'd obey. He turned toward his horse and mounted, thinking how much these men had changed. At least, they had changed in temper and resolve, but what they'd do when the shooting started was something else. Riley Rand obviously thought that one man like Smoke Kinnear was worth ten settlers, and Brad wondered if Rand was wrong.

Brad rode away, making a wide turn through the sagebrush so that he would come into Rand's camp from the north. A shot rang out, suddenly and without warning. Brad reined up, wondering if he had been seen. Then he realized that the shot had not been intended for him. It had been some distance to the north. He rode on, puzzled about it and unable to quiet the worry in him. Kinnear or Dollit might have met up with one of the settlers, Hildreth perhaps, and shot him down. If that had happened, there would be no holding the men at the fire.

The Rand fire was still too big. Covered by darkness, Brad reined up and sat his saddle for a few moments, watching. George McCloud was there. So was the Chinese cook. Apparently everyone else was gone, although it was quite likely that Gail was in her tent.

Again worry gnawed at Brad's nerves. He had thought Rand and his men would be here. If they intended to strike tonight, they would likely be in camp now, waiting until the small hours before dawn to make their raid. Now Brad saw that he had guessed wrong. To go back and get the settlers and then start hunting for Rand would be both futile and foolish. If only there was some way to find out exactly what Rand was planning. . . . An idea struck Brad. George McCloud might know, and he was a man who could be made to talk.

Dismounting, Brad moved silently toward the fire. The cook was working at the chuck wagon. McCloud was idling

75

by the fire, round-cheeked face untouched by worry or fear. He probably thought he was on a picnic, Brad thought. Maybe he wouldn't know. He didn't look like the kind of man who would have a part in Rand's scheming.

Brad moved in, gun palmed. McCloud heard him as he came into the firelight. He jumped up and whirled to face Brad, right hand grabbing for a gun in a shoulder holster.

"Stand pat," Brad ordered.

McCloud's hand fell away, and he began to curse in a low scared voice.

He knows, Brad thought. *He's into this up to his neck.*

At the moment Brad was watching McCloud, and it was exactly that moment when the Chinese cook wheeled and threw a butcher knife, the blade a bright flash of silver in the firelight. It missed by inches, and, when the cook saw he'd failed, he began to yell for mercy.

"Chang good now," he whimpered. "Belly good."

"You're darn' tootin' right you'll be good," Brad said angrily. "You make another funny move and I'll cut off your pigtail at your neck. Savvy?"

The cook bobbed his head up and down.

Brad motioned to McCloud. "Pull your gun and drop it. Try to use it and you'll be a goner."

Sullenly McCloud drew his gun and tossed it away.

Brad moved close to him. He said: "I'll have a look for a hide-out, friend. You ain't as harmless as you look."

Brad felt of McCloud with his left hand, right holding his gun, but there was no other weapon on the man. McCloud stood motionless, frowning with apprehension. When Brad stepped back, he demanded: "What do you want?"

"I'm looking for Rand and his bunch. Where are they?"

"I don't know."

76

"Who fired that shot I heard a while ago?"

"I don't know."

"When did Rand and his boys ride out?"

"About an hour ago."

"Gail go with them?"

"Yes."

"You knew that Cory Steele was murdered?"

"Nick Bailey said something about it."

"Nick do it?"

"I don't know."

"You don't know very much, do you?" Brad asked angrily.

McCloud shook his head. "That's right. I don't ask Rand about his plans."

"Maybe you know what you're doing here?"

Courage had drained back into McCloud now. He gave Brad a defiant grin. "Sure. I came to see the country. I'll tell you one thing, Wilder. Gail knows she made a mistake when she stopped Kinnear from shooting you the other night. She's just too soft-hearted for Riley. He's about ready to ship her back to Winnemucca, and then he'll clean this valley out."

"Maybe he'll ship you, too."

"Not me. I don't worry anybody. By fall I'll be ready to go back East and tell my friends some stories that will brand me the biggest liar on this side of the Atlantic."

"If you live long enough to go back," Brad said. "Maybe you *are* the biggest liar on this side of the Atlantic. What's Rand up to tonight?"

"I said I didn't know anything about it."

There was a chance Rand's bunch might ride in, and Brad didn't want to be caught here alone. He said: "I'm mighty sure you ain't here just to see the country. I'm

77

taking you along. Saddle up."

"Now see here, my man. . . ."

Brad motioned with his gun. "Don't think I'm your man, friend. You ain't in New York now. Saddle up."

For a moment McCloud stared at the gun in Brad's hand. He said: "I think you would kill me just like you'd shoot a . . . a. . . ."

"Rabbit," Brad said. "You're right, I would. Before the night's over you'll swing that tongue of yours, or I'll pull it out of your head. Move now."

McCloud obeyed, Brad backing away so that he could watch both the cook and McCloud. When the saddle was on and the cinch tightened, Brad said: "Climb up. My horse is out here a piece. Was I you, I wouldn't try to make a run for it. I shoot awful good in the dark."

McCloud made no answer. He rode slowly away from the fire, Brad walking beside him until he reached his horse. He said: "Pull up."

"Where we going?"

"Some of Cory's Steele's friends are waiting a piece east of here. They've got ropes for Dollit and Nick Bailey, but maybe your neck will fit one of the loops."

"You wouldn't do that. It would be murder."

"We've had a murder, and the man who got it was a better man than you'll ever be. All I want from you is a little talk."

"You forget who I am. My brother. . . ."

"It makes no difference if your brother is the king of Siam. Where's Rand?"

"I don't know."

Brad was in the saddle now, his gun still palmed. "Let's ride, and, while you're riding, you'd better do some thinking."

They rode eastward, McCloud saying nothing. There was a sort of sullen courage in him that surprised Brad, but he still thought the man would break. They came within sight of the fire in the pocket and turned toward it. As they rode into the light, the settlers crowded around them.

"Who's this yahoo?" O'Shay demanded.

"Calls himself McCloud. Says he's got a brother who's a big gun in the East, so we've got to go easy on him."

Al Benton laughed. "That's a good reason to go easy. What'd you fetch him along for, Brad?"

"Nobody was in camp but McCloud and the Chinese cook. I figured this jigger would know what Rand's up to."

There was a moment of shocked silence while they stared at Brad. He sensed the rising fear in them as they realized that Rand and his men were somewhere out in the valley. Benton whispered: "I didn't leave my family at Getalong like you said. They're in my cabin. You reckon Rand aims to . . . ?"

"You fool," Brad said angrily. "You feather-headed fool! I told you. . . ."

"Wait a minute, Brad," O'Shay cut in. "Somebody's coming."

Brad stepped down. "Stay there, McCloud. Everybody else get away from the fire."

They obeyed and stood motionless just outside the fringe of firelight while they waited, guns in their hands.

For that one tight moment there was no sound but the crackling of the fire and the whisper of horses' hoofs. McCloud sat his saddle beside the fire, paralyzed by fear, his round-cheeked face as pale as a dawn sky. Then Hildreth rode into view leading a horse, a man swaying in the saddle, and a whoop came out of half a dozen throats as tension drained out of the men.

"Why didn't you give a holler?" O'Shay called. "You just about had us spooked."

Then they saw that the other man was Nick Bailey, and they crowded up, Brad asking: "Where'd you find him?"

"He's hit bad," Hildreth said. "Heard him holler a couple of miles north of here. Found him lying in the grass. Dollit plugged him. Figured he'd killed him, I reckon."

Brad and Benton helped Bailey down and carried him to the fire. He'd been shot in the stomach and blood had made a dark stain on his shirt front. His eyes were open, and they fixed on Brad, empty now of the jealous hatred they had so often held when he'd looked at Brad. His face was a ghastly gray, and, when he coughed, a bloody froth touched his lips. He was very close to death.

Brad brought a saddle and blanket, lifted Bailey's head, and slid the saddle under it, then covered him with the blanket. Brad motioned for McCloud to get down. "Stay there," Brad ordered. "Savvy?"

McCloud stepped down, nodding, and moved to the other side of the fire. Bailey reached up and touched Brad's leg. He whispered: "Dad here?"

Kneeling beside Bailey, Brad said: "No."

"I'm glad. You figured on hanging me, didn't you, and you didn't want him to see it?"

"That's right, Nick," Hildreth said, kneeling on the other side of the dying man.

"Funny," Bailey whispered. "Now that it's too late, I can see a lot of things I never could before. Tell Dad I'm sorry for all the worry I caused him. Tell him I didn't kill Cory. Dollit did."

"Why?" Brad asked.

"Rand sent Dollit here last fall to spy on everybody. He's had his eyes on this valley for quite a while, but he had trouble raising the money. Then they met up with McCloud. Rand had the *dinero* then, but he ran into trouble in Salem making the deal." For a moment Bailey was silent, fighting the weakness that was taking hold of him. Then he said: "I'm cold. Inside." He clenched his fists, and looked at Brad. "I've hated you on account of Jeanie. She's loved you all the time. Maybe I never had a chance with her. Just thought I did. Dollit came along. Offered me a fortune to side him. That's why I sold out yesterday. Rand thought that, if two of us started it, everybody would sell out." His eyes closed.

Brad motioned to Benton. "Toss some more wood on the fire. He's shivering."

Benton obeyed, and a flame leaped up.

Bailey's eyes opened and sought Hildreth's face. "You've got to fight, Tom. Rand don't own the valley like he claims. Cory's deal went through. Dollit shot the mailman. That's why he never got in. There was a letter to Cory."

"We'll fight, Nick," Hildreth said softly. "You bet we'll fight."

"I didn't know Dollit aimed to beef Cory," Bailey went on. "He shot him before I saw what he was up to. Rand wanted Cory out of the way. Dollit told Rand that Cory and Wilder were the only ones who'd fight. Rand was awful mad at Gail for stopping Kinnear from killing Wilder. Next time they'll get him."

Bailey's eyes closed again, and for a moment Brad thought he was gone. Then he saw that Bailey was still breathing. His eyes fluttered open, and for a moment they moved wildly. "Wilder? You there? It's dark. I can't see you."

"I'm here." Brad laid a hand on Bailey's arm. "Right here."

"You've got to ride. Rand aims to burn some cabins to-night. He went loco after the meeting fizzled out. He'll kill anybody who tries to stop him. He's gonna burn the store, too. I couldn't stand it no longer. He'd have murdered my folks, too. I tried to stop 'em. Dollit . . . drilled . . . me." Bailey tried to say something more, but the words would not come. He coughed, and blood was a bright red stain on his lips. "I deserved what I got." His eyes were open, but they were staring unseeingly at the sky. "Wilder. It's awful dark. You there?"

"I'm still here."

"Take good care of Jeanie. Tell . . . my . . . folks. . . ."

That was all he could say. Brad felt of his wrist, but there was no flicker of a pulse. Brad drew the blanket over his face and rose. "You knew him better than I did, Tom. He couldn't go all the way with Dollit."

The men stirred. O'Shay said: "We've got some riding to do, Brad."

Brad nodded, eyes swinging around the half circle of men and coming to rest on McCloud who was still standing on the other side of the fire as if he had been frozen there. "You heard what he said about your giving Rand the money to buy the valley. That right?"

"Go chase yourself," McCloud said sullenly.

Brad drew his gun. "We ain't got time to fuss with you. I want an answer."

McCloud glanced down at Bailey's blanket-covered body, his mouth twitching. Then he raised his eyes to Brad. "Sure, that's right. It's my money Rand used to buy the herd that's coming up the trail, and it was my money he was going to use to buy the valley, but he won't need it now. We'll use the valley regardless."

Brad holstered his gun, and swung to the others. "Tom,

Swampland Empire

you and Malone fetch Bailey's body in. The rest of us have got to split the breeze getting to the store."

"Our families are there!" O'Shay cried. "If Rand. . . ."

"Stop worrying," Brad said. "Old man Bailey's there. I don't know about the rest of the women, but Jeanie's a good shot. Let's ride."

"My family went home," Al Benton whispered. He grabbed Brad's shoulder, pointing north with his other hand to a finger of flame that was leaping skyward. "Fire! That's my cabin."

Chapter Four

There was a flurry of action, tightening cinches, and mounting and reining horses away from the fire. There were bitter oaths and angry threats from men who had never been filled with a killing rage as they were now. At the moment danger lay miles away across the valley. They were not yet face to face with it. It would be different when they were, for in the end numbers would not make much difference. One man like Smoke Kinnear could stare the lot of them down. In spite of their talk, Brad was the one who would finally have to do the job. Cory, Brad thought, had foreseen that from the first.

Mounting, Brad called: "Rimrock, you ride with McCloud. We're going to need him before the night's over. See he don't get behind."

"I'm not a good rider," McCloud cried. "I can't keep up . . . !"

"You'll keep up," O'Shay bawled, "or you'll be laying belly down out in the sagebrush!"

Most of the settlers were already strung out toward the lake. Brad touched his horse up and came alongside Al Benton who was in the lead. The distance between Brad and Benton in front and the others behind gradually widened.

"Slow up!" Brad shouted. "You'll kill your horse the way you're riding."

"I don't care if I do," Benton shouted back in a ragged voice. "My wife and kids. . . ."

"Rand's ornery, but he ain't a woman-killer."

"You don't know. . . ."

"Take another look, Al. I'm guessing it's my cabin we're seeing."

Brad could not be sure at this distance, but Benton must have found relief in the thought, for he pulled his gelding down to a slower pace. They rode steadily toward the blaze across the long sweep of the valley that dropped gently northward, then they were out of the sagebrush and crossing the low flat that bordered the tule-fringed lake, moist soil that would, by fall, be covered with grass belly high on a horse. Cow paradise, just as Rand had said.

Brad thought of the women and children in Hildreth's house with only old Bailey to defend them. A few of the boys were old enough to use guns. Jeanie would do her part. He thought of Jeanie wounded, perhaps dying, and suddenly he was filled with a cold, relentless purpose that would carry him straight to Riley Rand.

Al Benton's voice beat against Brad's ears: "You're right. It's your place."

A few minutes later they reined up in Brad's yard and sat their saddles, staring at the smoldering coals that had been a cabin. It had taken a lot of work to build that cabin and the few pieces of crude furniture. Everything was gone except the clothes Brad had on.

Benton cursed in a low, flat tone, but Brad felt little emotion. This was a minor thing. The big job waited to be done, and time was running out. Others rode in now and reined up to blow their horses. Brad hipped around in his saddle, calling: "McCloud, this your idea?"

"No."

"You said it was your investment that fetched Rand up here. Don't you call the turn?"

"No. Rand bargained for a free hand before we left Winnemucca. I told you I just came for the trip."

"Then you're a damned fool to put your money out and let the other fellow blow it the way he wants to."

"Maybe I am," McCloud shouted, "but Riley promised me a ranch! A big ranch! An empire! You understand? The way he carries out his promise is his business."

"An empire," Brad breathed. "A swampland empire, and you'll wear the crown. That's it, ain't it, McCloud?"

"That's it."

"Before we're done, maybe we *will* hang you. Al, hike out for home. There's enough of us to do this chore without you."

Without a word Benton whirled his horse and rode westward around the lake. Brad reined the other way, half expecting flames to burst up from the Steele cabin, but when he saw a fire a few minutes later, it was the Widow Bain's place, not the Steele cabin. Rand, Brad guessed, had saved Jeanie's place because it was the best house in the valley. It was likely that Rand planned to use it as the headquarters of McCloud's ranch until a bigger place could be built.

Rand had ridden past four cabins tonight and burned three. He intended to wipe Hildreth out, confident that the settlers, understanding the kind of man they were up against, would run. If they were still stubborn, their cattle would go. If that didn't work, there would be more killings. Gail, Brad thought, had lost any influence she'd ever held over her brother. If Rand lived, there could be no turning back for him.

Getalong was directly ahead. It would not have surprised Brad to have seen Hildreth's buildings burning. But there was no light to brighten the blackness except that from a lamp in the back of Hildreth's house.

One moment there was silence except for the usual night sounds, then gunfire broke out, a single burst, and after that a man's shout.

Exultation swept through Brad. Riley Rand had run into more than he had bargained for. Old man Bailey and the women and kids were fighting. Rand had made a wrong guess, perhaps a fatal one, when he had taken the settlers so lightly. He should have had an army of gunslingers instead of just Smoke Kinnear and Whang Dollit. Courage, like gold, is where you find it, and the men coming behind Brad might be encouraged by this show of strength in a way Rand had not counted on.

He was close to Hildreth's house now, calling: "It's Brad! Hold your fire!"

The back door swung open. Lamplight spilled out across the grass. The Widow Bain cried: "Hurry, Brad, hurry. We've been looking for you."

Brad pulled his sweat-gummed horse to a stop and swung down. There were a number of women and several children in the back of the house, and the fury grew in him. What a hell of a thing this was—Rand's endangering the lives of these people.

They were a scared lot. Only the Widow Bain seemed self-possessed. She patted Brad's shoulder, saying: "You're a sight for sore eyes, boy. You can take over the fighting now, and welcome to it."

"Where're the others?" a woman cried. "Where's my husband?"

"Everybody's all right."

Brad pushed through the crowd, seeking Jeanie, but she wasn't here. The widow kept close behind him, saying: "If it hadn't been for Jeanie, we'd have walked out of here, and Rand would have burned everything, but that Jeanie's just like her dad. She's a fighter right down to her toes."

Brad went on to the front room. Old man Bailey was there with a bloody rag tied around his head. The oldest Bain kid was crouched behind a window, a six-gun in his hand, left arm in a sling. Then Brad saw Jeanie near another window, a Winchester in her hands, blood streaming down her face from an open gash on her cheek.

"Jeanie!" Brad cried. "Jeanie."

When she saw it was Brad, a light burst across her face. "Brad!"

She dropped the Winchester and ran to him. He put his arms around her and held her close.

"Brad, are you all right?"

"Sure. Those yahoos gave us the slip. I figured we'd find them in camp. Looks like we should have stayed right here."

She wiped a hand across her face. "A piece of glass from the window gave me a scratch. Nobody's hurt badly."

He looked at the gash. "Pretty deep." He nodded at the Widow Bain. "Better clean this up. May leave a scar."

"It doesn't matter," Jeanie said impatiently. "They've been threatening to rush us. They're holed up in the store."

"They've got a bear by the tail now." Brad grinned at her. "They won't do any rushing. You know what you've done tonight?"

"Done?" She shook her head. "We haven't done anything."

"You've done quite a chore," Brad said. "You've showed

Rand that women and kids and one old man will fight. He can't lick us now, Jeanie, not in a million years. I wish Cory could see this."

Jeanie said gravely: "He's right here with us. If he hadn't been, we'd have quit when they rode up."

Some of the men were riding in. They crowded into the kitchen, O'Shay keeping his gun on McCloud.

"Damn that Rand!" O'Shay bellowed. "He burned our cabin. Everything we own went up in smoke. Burned yours, too, Missus Bain."

Mrs. O'Shay began to cry hysterically, but the Widow Bain only spread her hands and said: "Then we'll have to build again."

O'Shay prodded McCloud in the back with his gun. "You'll pay us for every bit of devilment this Rand *hombre* has done since he hit the valley."

Old man Bailey pushed his way into the crowded kitchen, calling: "Nick, Nick? He wasn't with Rand's bunch. Have any of you seen him?"

Hildreth could have told him if he were here, but Hildreth would not be in for hours, so Brad told the old man as gently as he could, adding: "I can't blame him for hating me or loving Jeanie. He took the wrong road, but when the last chip was down, he found out he couldn't go all the way with Dollit."

Mrs. Bailey was crying, but the old man drew himself erect, a defiant pride in his eyes. "If Nick had to die, I'm glad he went that way. He didn't forget his people."

"That's right," Brad said.

"What's going on here?" O'Shay demanded imperiously. "Who's in the store?"

"Rand and his sister," Jeanie said. "Dollit and that gunman Kinnear are with them. They rode up in front and

89

told us to get out of the house. They said they were going to burn the house and the store."

"You know why we didn't go?" the Widow Bain demanded. "Because Jeanie wouldn't let us. She grabbed a Winchester and put a hole through Rand's bonnet. You should have seen 'em scurry."

"They came through the back of the store," Jeanie said, "and now they're forted up behind the front windows. About every half hour Rand has been asking us if we're ready to get out."

"You men are here." The Widow Bain motioned toward the store. "Six, seven, eight of you with Bailey. Go run 'em out and get this over with."

No one moved. O'Shay shifted uneasily. "You're forgetting one thing, Missus Bain. Them three in there are mighty tough hands. They'd cut us down before we got halfway across the yard."

"There's enough of us to do the job," Brad said. "It's still dark. We could get to the front door of the store, all right."

"Suppose we did?" O'Shay asked loudly. "We'd go in and they'd be in the dark and what light there is would be behind us. We'd be targets for 'em."

They wouldn't back him. They had blown hot and cold, and now they were cold. Knowing that Cory Steele's murderer was in the store and knowing that three cabins had been burned this night, the fury had died in them.

"I'm ashamed of you," Jeanie cried. "You know what Dad would do if he was here."

"And you know what Brad will do now," the Widow Bain said in high contempt. "Come on, Brad. Give me your gun, Rimrock. I'll side him."

"I'll go," Bailey said quickly.

"It won't do!" O'Shay shouted. "No use getting burned down for nothing. We'll wait 'em out."

"We can't do that," Brad said. "It's almost dawn now. Unless we bottle 'em up in the store, they'll ride out after a while. Then we'd have to run 'em down again. This is the best chance we'll ever have."

McCloud laughed. "You're a bunch of fools to think you could lick Rand. You know what he said?"

"I don't care what he said!" O'Shay shouted defiantly. "We'll sit him out."

"I'll tell you," McCloud went on. "When Dollit told us how it stacked up here in the valley, Riley said Smoke Kinnear was worth all of you. Burn a few cabins, throw a few slugs, and you'd run like chickens when a hawk flies over the barnyard."

"Damn you!" O'Shay slapped the man across the face. "You'd like to get us out there in the yard so they could smoke us down. Well, we ain't going. We'll sneak around to the back of the store and bottle 'em up. Sooner or later they'll come out."

McCloud stepped back, raising a hand to his cheek. He said: "It took a brave man to do that, O'Shay, holding a gun in your hand like you are."

Some of the rest had ridden up and were crowding in through the back door. It wouldn't make any difference, Brad knew. They had not accepted him.

"All right, Rimrock," Brad said. "I'll do the job, me and McCloud."

"Not me!" McCloud cried in sudden fear. "I'm on the other side. Remember?"

"You ain't on either side," Brad said bluntly, "which is something you never figured out. Riley Rand don't give a damn about you if he's got your money to buy the valley. He has got it, ain't he?"

For a moment McCloud was silent, then he blurted: "Yes, he has the money, but Gail and I are engaged to be married. That makes it different."

Brad shook his head. "You haven't had any experience with fellows like Riley Rand. I have. If Gail's idea of buying us out had worked, it would be different, but we didn't sell. Now Rand will bull it through his way."

"Brad." It was Bud Bain, calling from the front room. "Rand's hollering at us."

McCloud forced a laugh. "Better go see about it, Wilder. I'm not worried."

"You'd better be." Turning, Brad walked to the door. He shouted: "What's on your mind, Rand?"

"We're done waiting!" Rand called. "Everybody that's in the house walk out or we'll burn the store."

"We've got McCloud," Brad said. "If you burn the store, he's a dead duck."

"No!" Gail screamed.

Rand's answer was a flurry of shots. Brad dropped flat on his stomach as slugs whined through the doorway.

When the echoes of the shots died, Rand called: "We're giving you half an hour! Then the store goes. We'll burn every cabin in the valley and run your stock out. Now will you make a deal?"

"What kind of a deal?"

"We'll hold off till sundown if you'll agree to get your stuff out of the valley by then. That's the best we'll do."

"No!" Gail screamed. "We'll. . . ."

She never finished. Rand, Brad guessed, had clapped his hand over her mouth.

"You boys give McCloud and me about fifteen minutes," Brad said to those with him. "Then throw all the slugs you can against the front of the store."

Jeanie gripped his arm. "What are you going to do?"

"McCloud and me will go around to the back. We'll finish this now."

"The hell I will," McCloud breathed. "You're licked, and you know it."

"No, I don't know it." Brad motioned to O'Shay. "You boys are sure bent on living to a ripe old age. I want to know just one thing. Will you scatter out on both sides of the house and throw some lead?"

"Yes," O'Shay said. "We'll do that."

"Wait," McCloud said. "Wait now. Use your head. You're a long ways from any source of supplies. Suppose Riley burns the store? What will you live off?"

"Tom has a wagon of supplies coming," Mrs. Hildreth said in a low voice. "We'll make out. Go ahead, Brad."

He looked at her, surprised. He had thought she would be the last person in the house to say that. Perhaps it was because her husband was not here. If the fight could be finished before Tom Hildreth came, he would not be killed. It was not courage, he saw then. She was simply looking out for her man. The store meant little to her. Brad Wilder's life meant less, for if Brad were killed, there would be no more resistance.

"Don't count on that wagon," McCloud said.

"Why not?" Mrs. Hildreth demanded.

"Dollit and Nick Bailey stopped it several days ago in the mountains," McCloud answered. "They killed the driver and burned the wagon."

They cried out, some of them, for they had all known Hildreth was expecting the load of supplies. Mrs. Bailey bowed her head, but old Bailey drew himself erect again, desperately trying to hold onto his self-respect.

"I'll go with you, Brad," Bailey said. "It's too much for one man."

"There's me and McCloud," Brad said. "You get back to that window. I can count on you and Jeanie and Bud Bain to throw some slugs. I ain't sure I can count on anyone else."

"We'll do it," O'Shay said loudly.

"I won't have no part in it," McCloud bellowed. "Which side do you think . . . ?"

"You'll do it." Brad drew his gun and lined it on McCloud. "Move."

McCloud turned, and the crowd opened a path for him. They walked out, Brad a pace behind McCloud, and, when they were outside, Brad discovered that Jeanie had followed him.

She asked: "Must it always be you, Brad?"

"I reckon," he said. "You hike back to the front of the house. McCloud, get down on your belly. That's the way we're traveling to the back of the store. Then you're gonna be my shield. We'll see how good you stand with Riley Rand."

It took them ten minutes to worm their way to the rear of the store.

Brad said: "If you want to live long enough to see the sun come up, you'd better keep quiet. They'd as soon plug you as anybody else."

McCloud made no answer. They went on through the grass, the dawn light deepening a little. It was touch and go, and Brad knew it. He was gambling that Rand's party was in the front of the store, that Rand would not expect the fight to be brought to him. Then, thinking of the way the

94

settlers had backed down, it seemed to Brad that Rand's judgment of the settlers had been all too accurate. Coldly realistic now, Brad knew exactly how long the odds were against him.

With time running out, he thought of Cory Steele and the faith Cory had had in him. That was the real reason he was here on his belly crawling through the grass. It was as if Cory were here with him, telling him that only a few lead but many follow, that this was a good job worth the doing, the job Cory had died for.

Brad could accept all of that now. Within these last few days he had come to believe in a new set of values. Idealistic, perhaps a little crazy, but the kind of values that made a man feel good inside, that gave the future a meaning it had never held for him before.

McCloud stopped. He said: "Go ahead. Shoot me. I'm not going on."

"Move," Brad whispered. "Damn you, move. Don't make me beef you out here like a rabbit."

"Go ahead," McCloud said again. "My luck's all used up. You're right about Riley. He's got my money, and he'd just as soon kill me as not."

Brad's face was close to McCloud's. In the thin dawn light he saw in the Easterner's expression the resignation that comes from a sense of final and utter failure.

"I'll tell you how it is," McCloud said in a rush of words as if he wanted to say this before it was too late. "I've been a big man's baby brother. I've had to bow and scrape and take a back seat. I wasn't man enough to play the Wall Street game, so I told my brother I'd make my own way out here. That's why I threw in with Rand."

"Get on your feet," Brad whispered.

But there was nothing now that could stop McCloud's

flow of words. "I love Gail. I came out here looking for a ranch and met Gail in Winnemucca. Then I met Riley and he told me he knew just the spot. I gave him the money to buy the herd and hire a crew. I gave him more to buy the valley, but something went wrong in Salem, and the deal didn't go through. That's why we sent Dollit up here last fall. Rand said we'd come on regardless and to hell with the state. If we had the valley, they'd have to sell to us. You see how it is, Wilder. I'm not worth a damn. Not back East or out here. I had to depend on a man like Riley Rand. . . ."

"This is no time to gab," Brad said hotly. "We're going through that door."

Brad was on his feet, gun in his right hand, his left gripping McCloud's coat collar. That was when the fifteen minutes were up. Firing broke out from the house, heavy firing that came from ten or twelve Colts and Winchesters. There must have been a shotgun or two, and it sounded as if someone had grabbed Tom Hildreth's old buffalo gun off the wall and was using it.

Somehow Brad got McCloud to his feet, and he lifted a knee to the seat of the man's pants. He shouted: "Get through that door! Damn you and your talk." He shoved his gun muzzle into the soft fat over McCloud's ribs. "I aimed to be going through the door when the shooting started."

Whimpering, McCloud ran toward the door, Brad crowding behind him. The back door was locked. Brad shot the lock off and kicked the door open. The light was behind them as they crowded into the back room, and Smoke Kinnear, running in from the store, let go with a shot that knocked McCloud off his feet.

There was so little light inside the store building that Kinnear's shape was only a vague blur in front of Brad as he threw a shot at the gunman and lunged sideways out of the doorway.

"Gail!" McCloud screamed. "Gail, he shot me! Gail! Gail . . . !" His last word was drowned by another report. Kinnear, coming into the back room, had shot McCloud a second time.

Gail must have followed Kinnear, for Brad saw the flash of fire from a small revolver. It was directly behind the gunman. Then the shadowy bulk of his body was gone, and Gail was running toward McCloud, screaming: "George! Where are you, George?"

Another man loomed behind her, a squat massive shape. Whang Dollit! Brad fired and dropped behind a cracker barrel. He heard the other shoot, the slug ripping into the wall. Brad, poking his head around the barrel, caught Dollit's square body in his sights, squeezed the trigger, and saw Dollit spill forward on his face.

There was a lull in the firing from the house. Rand's gun was silent, too, but he was out there, somewhere in the front of the store.

The shooting started again. Brad thumbed shells into the cylinder of his gun and crawled forward, keeping low. Gail was behind him.

Brad reached the store and went on, hugging the floor. He could not see Rand, could not hear him. It was possible that the man had been tagged by a stray bullet, but Brad could not count on such luck. He worked his way around the end of the pine counter. Still he could not see Rand.

The minutes dragged by, each of them an eternity to Brad. He laid belly flat on the floor, gun in his right hand. The firing continued, riddling the front of the store. He moved forward again, knowing he couldn't let this go on. Gail was a potential danger behind him. Rand's nerves might crack under this pressure. If he started firing wildly and kept his bullets low, Brad was likely to stop one of them.

Then Brad's left hand, reaching forward as he crawled, touched some tools that Hildreth had left leaning against the wall. Another lull came in the firing. Brad carefully picked up a shovel and tossed it over the counter. The sound of it hitting the floor was nerve-shattering in this interlude of quiet, and it accomplished exactly what Brad wanted. Rand, hidden directly in front of Brad behind a low pile of sugar sacks, let go a shot.

Brad brought himself upright and lunged forward, firing as he moved. Now he could see Rand. His first shot must have been a clean miss, for Rand threw a bullet that seared his left side. It was the one chance Rand had, and he decreed his own death when he failed to stop Brad.

Rand was motionless, a still target, and Brad was moving. He was close now, and he shot three times, fast, and Rand thudded to the floor, gun falling from slack fingers.

"All right, all right!" Brad called. "Hold your fire!"

They came rushing across the yard toward the store, Jeanie and old man Bailey and Bud Bain. Rimrock O'Shay was with them, talking big now that the fight was over, and Tom Hildreth was there, panting after the short run.

"I'm not hurt much," Brad said at once in answer to Jeanie's alarmed question. "Just lost a little meat along my ribs. Come on. Gail's back here."

Brad ran along the counter, Jeanie a step behind him, the others trailing. O'Shay shouted: "Rand's dead!" He stumbled over Dollit's body, and then he saw Kinnear.

Gail was on her feet, tall and straight-backed. She said tonelessly: "George is dead."

Brad took her by the shoulders and shoved her through the door, saying: "I'm sorry about McCloud, but if it hadn't been for him, this wouldn't have happened."

She pushed Brad's hands away from her. "I don't need your sympathy, Wilder," she said evenly. "Riley was right about everybody in the valley. If I had let Kinnear kill you that first night, it wouldn't have gone this way."

"She's one of 'em," O'Shay blurted. "I don't see why we don't. . . ."

"Shut up," Brad said, "or I'll work that ugly mug of yours over till even your own wife won't recognize you."

O'Shay subsided at once.

Gail said: "He'd do it, mister. You meet up with one man like Wilder in about ten million. It was our bad luck to run into him here."

"You can go, miss," Hildreth said. "No one will lay a hand on you."

"I'm to thank you, I suppose." She looked at Jeanie, frowning. "Well, this is justice after what happened to your father. I have no tears for my brother. This was robbery that he planned, and he deserved what he got. I tried to stop him, but I couldn't."

"There was a letter . . . ," Brad began.

"You'll find it in Riley's coat pocket. You own the valley, Miss Steele. You can give your people the homes your father talked about, the little people that let Brad Wilder do their fighting for them."

She turned and would have walked away if Brad had not said: "If you need some help. . . ."

She swung back, angry. "I don't need any help. Chang and I will take the wagons back down the trail. I've still got the herd. I'll find a place for it somewhere."

This time Brad let her go. He took Jeanie's hand, and

they walked toward the lake.

Jeanie said: "You're hurt. You'd better. . . ."

"It'll wait. I've got something to say. Been trying to say it ever since I saw you, but I got all balled up. I kept telling myself I'd wait till I got my place to going, but I can't wait any longer. You need me and I sure need you. I always will."

"I guess it was just as well that you waited," she said. "I just didn't want to grow up, but after Nick came out that time and tried to use his gun. . . ." She paused, staring across the lake. "Well, I knew then, Brad, I knew, and I wondered why I hadn't known all the time."

Brad turned Jeanie to face him and kissed her, and the kiss, like the morning, was filled with promise.

"Funny," he said softly as he put a tip of a finger against her freckled nose. "The first time I saw you I thought you were pretty, but now you look downright beautiful."

Wheels Roll West

Chapter One

By three in the afternoon Jim Horn had located a suitable camp ground along the Arkansas River, just below where Lost Creek came tumbling in from the south. He turned back downriver, riding slowly, for there was no hurry now. Tomorrow the Ohio to Colorado colony would make the last day's journey up the creek to Lost Valley and Horn's job would be finished. Angus Morgan would pay him off tonight, probably without even a thank you, and he'd ride on just as he had been riding on for most of his twenty-eight years.

Well, it was all right. There were plenty of opportunities in Colorado for a man if he wanted to look for them. But maybe he didn't. Maybe he was the proverbial rolling stone that never gathered any moss. It had always been fun to keep rolling, and there was a lot of country he hadn't seen. But now he'd met Ruth Morgan.

He rounded a turn in the river and saw her riding toward him, tall and straight in the saddle, the most graceful woman he had ever seen. He reined up to wait for her, wondering how she had managed to get away from her father's wagon that she had been driving. He wondered, too, why his heart began to pound.

Foolish! Just plain damned foolish! Like a kid falling in

love for the first time. He was too old to act like this. He'd traveled alone too long to lose his head over a woman. But Ruth Morgan was a very special woman, good-looking and strong and filled with a great vitality. Much of the time she seemed as cool and distant as a glittering star in a black sky.

She rode up to him, smiling, and asked: "Find a good place?"

He held his answer for a moment, his eyes fixed on her. Her hat dangled down her back from a chin strap, and her black hair, carefully pinned up that morning, was now wind-ruffled and loose. Her brown eyes met his, and he sensed the restlessness that was in her, the discontent of a woman who was still sampling life and had not yet found what she wanted.

Nodding, he jerked a thumb upstream. "About a quarter of a mile from here."

"Shade?"

He nodded again. "Some big cottonwoods."

"Let's have a look," she said, and swung upriver.

He reined his black gelding in beside the girl, glancing sideways at her. Viewed from the side, her chin was a little defiant. Looking at her this way, he was unable to see the dimple that he knew was there. Jim thought back to the spring day in Fort Wallace when Ruth's father, Angus Morgan, had asked him to guide the colony to Lost Valley and decided he'd been a chuckle-headed idiot for saying yes. Sure, he'd been out of a job at the time, but being out of a job had never worried him. Looking at it now with cool objectivity, he knew he would not have taken the job if he had not met Ruth Morgan and known that she would be going with the colony.

She glanced at him, frowning. "What's the matter, my face dirty?"

"No. I'm just taking a good look. Sort of wanted to put a picture of it in my mind."

The frown faded out. "Why?"

"In an hour or so your dad will pay me off. Don't reckon I'll be seeing you any more, and I wanted to remember what you looked like."

She gave him a pleased smile. "I'm surprised, Jim. I didn't think you were interested in anything but camping places and water holes and grass for the stock and such."

She was looking straight ahead again, her chin tilted more defiantly than usual. No, it wouldn't do. He'd best forget her. She wasn't the kind who would ride over the nearest hill just to see what was there. She'd find a spot along the river she liked and she'd stay: *Let's build a cabin here and you plow the ground and raise a crop. After a while other folks will come and you'll be rich and respectable, and I'll go to church and be president of the Ladies' Aid.* Well, that wasn't for Jim Horn. Not by a jug full!

"I always figured a man was a fool to reach for what he couldn't have," he said.

"How do you know you can't have it?" she demanded. "If you think I'm engaged to Rusty Hancock. . . ." She stopped as if not quite sure whether she was or not.

Horn said: "Rusty figures you are. I'll bet he's driving your wagon right now so you could take a ride."

"Well, suppose he is?" The chin was definitely defiant. "I never told Rusty I'd marry him. Besides, he's just a kid."

He was that, all right, Horn thought. Not yet twenty-one, Rusty Hancock had the look of a potato sprout that had grown too fast—a lot of bone but not much meat. Ruth wasn't any older, but she had matured. She had the right curves in the right places, balanced up as pretty as if the Lord had given her His special attention, and Horn had a feeling that she possessed all the desires and passions that a man wanted his woman to have.

"Rusty might be worth waiting for," Horn said. "Your pa kind o' favors him."

"It's just that his folks were Dad's friends," she said quickly, "and he has Rusty's money to invest. I . . . I. . . ." She bit her lip. "I shouldn't have said that. Nobody knows about it but Dad and Rusty and me."

"And Webb."

"Oh, no. Dad wouldn't talk . . . wouldn't tell him."

"Gold enough to build a big, purty place up yonder in Lost Valley." Horn shook his head. "Crazy dreaming. Your whole outfit is like a bunch of children. Why in thunder didn't they stay in Ohio?"

"Because there's opportunity in Colorado," she flung at him. "Because people working together can perform miracles." She stopped and looked at him accusingly. "You don't believe any of those things, do you?"

"No. I mean, yes, but there's one thing the West taught me a long time ago. A man who's worth a damn stands on his two legs, and he doesn't depend on his neighbors giving him a third one."

"You mean Dad. I know you don't think we'll make a go of it. Right from the day we left Fort Wallace you told Dad we wouldn't."

He shrugged. "That's just my notion. Angus Morgan's is something else. Look like he's got the ideas and Rusty's putting up the *dinero*."

The defiance had gone out of her. She said somberly: "That's about it. Stay with us, Jim. We're going to need you."

They had reached the camping place, and Horn reined up. "This is it," he said.

Ruth looked at the grassy bench above the Arkansas, at the giant cottonwoods and the cool patch of shade surrounded by dazzling sunlight, and then she glanced at the river, running high and cold now in late spring. "It's a pretty place," she murmured, and swung out of the saddle.

He stepped down, leaving the reins dangling. He stood close to her, a full head taller, his hair, as light as new rope, falling to his shoulders. He rubbed his hands along his dirty buckskins, thinking that this was the first time in all the weeks they had spent at Fort Wallace getting ready and in the passage across the wind-chilled Kansas and Colorado plains that Ruth had shown any real interest in him. Now she turned, her face lifted to his.

"I'm afraid, Jim." She put a hand on his arm. "I don't know why, but I'm afraid."

"You ought to be. Trouble is your dad knows so much he doesn't need any advice."

She stepped away from him, her eyes turning upstream. "I know. He's just too smart for his good or anyone else's. He's always been that way."

It was the first time he had heard her say that she understood Angus Morgan's weakness, for a weakness it was. He had gathered the colonists from the farms and small towns of southern Ohio, painting a rosy picture of their future in Colorado. He had sent Ike Webb, a one-man locating committee, to select their future homes, and Webb had picked Lost Valley. It was a poor choice, but when Horn had tried to tell Morgan that before they had left Fort Wallace, the colony leader had blown up.

"Webb has seen the valley," Morgan had shouted, "and I trust Ike Webb's judgment when it comes to land! Your job is to get us there. That's all. Just get us there."

Horn had not mentioned it again. It was their money

107

they were spending, their time and their labor, and the broken dreams would be theirs, too. If they had enough money to live through the first hard years, they might in time learn how to farm the high valley with its hard winters and short summers. Horn had never inquired about the colonists' financial backlog, but he was reasonably certain from talk he'd heard that they expected to raise a crop this year. If they didn't, they'd starve the following winter. And there was Newt Kimmel who would not stand for a bunch of greenhorns swarming all over his Clawhammer range.

There was nothing right about this thing. Angus Morgan was honest enough, but he was a pig-headed fool. If young Rusty Hancock wanted to throw his money away at Morgan's say-so, that was Rusty's business. He was young and strong, and he could start again, but it was different with the rest of them. Middle-aged men with families, farmers and craftsmen of one kind or another, they had taken Morgan's word, and they'd lose their shirts. The shirts might not be much, but when they were all people had, it was a hell of a bad thing.

Horn pulled Ruth around to face him. He said: "This isn't any of my business, which same your dad is going to tell me, but I hate to go off and leave a band of sheep in the same pasture with a pack of wolves."

"What are you getting at, Jim?"

"These people are licked before they get to Lost Valley. Maybe your dad would listen to you. Get 'em to go north where a farmer can raise something."

She stood very close to him, her face grave. "Jim, Jim, I'm just a woman. Men never listen to women."

"You're a mighty pretty one," he said, "and men listen to pretty women."

"Then why don't you listen to me? Stay with us, Jim.

108

The wolves won't bother the sheep if you're around."

There was nothing cold or distant about her now. Her lips, red and full, were parted, the smile lingering at their corners. Impulsively he pulled her to him and kissed her, holding her hard against his body, kissed her thoroughly and passionately. Her arms came up around his neck, and she clung to him, and, when he let her go, she still clung to him, her head against his chest.

"Jim, you were such a long time getting around to that," she whispered. "It isn't up to the woman to do the chasing, you know. That's a man's job."

He stared down at her, fighting a sudden rush of panic. The next thing he knew he'd be married, and she'd be wanting him to stay with the colony, she'd want him tied up to something that had been bound to fail from the beginning.

"I wasn't thinking about chasing or anything," he said lamely. "I mean, I'm not one to settle down, and you aren't the kind who'd follow me all over the country."

She stepped back, her face red. "All right, Mister Horn, so you aren't the kind to settle down. Well, a kiss doesn't mean anything to me, either."

"It isn't that," he said quickly. "It's just that I'm not sticking with this here colony, and you wouldn't go with me."

Horn had not heard Angus Morgan and Ike Webb ride up, and he was not aware of their presence until Morgan's big voice boomed out: "I've got one question to ask you, Horn. What are your intentions regarding my daughter?"

Horn wheeled, red-faced. "Right now I don't have any intentions."

Morgan stepped down from the saddle. He was a big man, tall, broad of shoulder, impressive-appearing with his dark, piercing eyes and heavy black beard. He had the look and bearing of a leader, but actually his talent for leadership had never been put to the test. Now, meeting the big man's eyes, Horn wondered how much of Morgan's swagger was skin-deep.

"I saw you kissing her," Morgan boomed. "Rusty Hancock considers himself engaged to her, and I favor Rusty. I know him. I don't know you. Sometimes I think you're half savage."

"And I ought to go live with the Utes." Horn motioned to the narrow cañon through which Lost Creek tumbled northward to meet the Arkansas. "There's your route to Lost Valley. Give me my two hundred dollars and I'll be riding."

Ruth had been listening, saying nothing. Now she walked toward her father, her head held high. "I made him kiss me," she said, "because I favor him. We need him, all of us."

"We don't need him," Ike Webb said in his blustering voice. "We're only one day's journey from the valley. Pay him off, Angus."

"Sure," Horn said softly. "Let Webb take you up the cañon."

"Don't think I can't!" Webb cried. "We didn't need you in the first place, and we don't need you now. Ruth's just silly about your damned long hair."

Horn liked almost everyone in the colony. He respected people who had no illusions about themselves and who were willing to take a gamble to better their conditions, but he disliked Morgan because of his conceit, and he distrusted Ike Webb. Webb was a short, squat man with a shrewd, animal-like cunning in his green eyes that made Horn wary of him. Actually he had no grounds for his suspicions beyond the fact that Webb had picked Lost Valley.

"I'm kind of curious about you, Webb," Horn said.

"What do you mean by that?" Webb demanded.

"I think you're a crook," Horn answered,

Webb swore, and his right hand dug for his gun, but at that moment his horse began to pitch, and Webb, caught by surprise with his gun half drawn, was thrown to the ground. He sat up, spluttering, his dignity injured more than his body, and found himself looking into Horn's .45.

"You're a fool, Webb," Horn said evenly. "You try that with someone else and they'll be digging a hole to plant you in."

"All right, all right now!" Morgan shouted. "Put your guns up. No need of trouble. You were out of line, Horn, and I'll hear no more of it. I've told you many times that I trust Webb implicitly."

"And that makes you the fool," Horn said hotly. "Give me my pay and I'll get the hell out of here."

"No." Ruth slipped her arm through Horn's as if to hold him against his will, defiant eyes on her father. "Jim knows this country, Dad. Listen to him."

"I'll listen to nobody. I'm the president of this colony." Morgan stroked his beard, gaze swinging to Ruth and back to Horn. Then he said grudgingly: "All right, Horn. Stay with us till we reach the valley."

"The hell I will. The agreement we made was for me to fetch you to the mouth of Lost Creek. You're here."

"I'll give you fifty dollars to stay with us till we reach the valley," Morgan said heavily.

Ruth's arm tightened against Horn's. She whispered: "Please, Jim. One more day. For me."

Horn hesitated, and then against his better judgment he said: "All right, one more day." He would not have done this for anyone but Ruth.

He walked toward his horse, deeply troubled. He had always been contemptuous of a man who surrendered his independence of mind to a woman. Now he had done exactly that.

The wagons came rolling around the point, young Rusty Hancock in the lead driving the Morgan wagon. Horn staked out his horse close to the base of the hill and, walking back to the river, watched the wagons come, swaying canvas tops dirty and weather-stained, horses sweat-gummed and thinned down by the countless miles they had traveled.

Horn hunkered at the river's edge, rolled a smoke, and fired it as he thought idly of his drifting years. He'd served with the Colorado volunteers at the battle of Glorietta Pass when the West had been saved for the Union. He'd done a number of things since—hunted buffalo for a railroad, ridden for Newt Kimmel's Clawhammer in Lost Valley, and carried a star in one of the Colorado mining camps. He'd even had a shot at mining.

Jack-of-all-trades, Horn thought bitterly, a drifter who placed his own freedom of movement and spirit above everything else. In a way he envied the stolid men with small ambitions, men content to settle down and fight the elements in the hope of eventually owning their homes, men who married and raised a flock of dirty-faced kids and were satisfied to sleep with their wives in one-room shacks and eat salt side and beans.

There were the others, the ambitious ones like Angus Morgan who dreamed king-size dreams. There were the Ike Webbs who flattered the ambitious ones, shrewd, scheming men who usually came out ahead in the end, their pockets filled with the gold of the men they flattered. It took all kinds to make the world, Horn thought as he watched the colonists make camp for the night. There was the usual clatter and rustle, the running and calling from one wagon to another, the laughter and shouts of children as they raced along the riverbank. Wood smoke rose from a dozen cook fires. There was the smell of it and the smell of coffee and frying bacon that made a man remember his belly was empty.

People like these colonists had settled the West. There had been the go-backs who had failed during the hard days following the first gold rush to Colorado, there had been the others who had stayed and bucked it through. Many of them had done well. It all depended on what was in a man, and Horn wondered about these people. Were they the go-backs of a later generation, or did they have what it took to hang and rattle? He didn't know. Only the pressure of time and privation would tell.

The restlessness grew in Horn until his nerves were trigger tight. He watched Ruth working at her cook fire, saw Morgan talking to Ike Webb who was flaring back and pounding a fist against the palm of his hand. He saw lank Rusty Hancock care for Morgan's horses, and then come stalking toward him. From the look on the boy's bony face, Jim knew this could be trouble.

Rusty came up and hunkered beside him. He said: "I want to talk to you, Horn." The boy rolled a cigarette, his hands trembling a little. "I know you can kill me and I sure as hell ain't no ring-tailed wowser when it comes to guns or knives, but just the same I'm fixing to tell you what you are."

Horn studied the boy's taut face. The sun was down now, and the cool of early evening was settling upon the cañon bottom. Rusty took off his hat and laid it beside him, reddish hair tousled. He was tall and ungainly from growing too fast; his long nose and long chin gave his face a sharp-featured look. The makings of a man were in him. Given time, he'd do, but now he was a little wild with the brashness of youth, and Horn considered it a bad gamble to bet on his reaching old age.

"Go ahead," Horn repeated. "I always wondered what I was."

Rusty fired his cigarette, staring at Horn through the smoke with grim belligerence. He said: "Angus said he caught you kissing Ruth."

"I kissed her," Horn said, "but there wasn't no getting caught about it."

"She's spoken for," Rusty said. "We growed up together in Ohio. My family lived next to the Morgans. I've loved her as long as I can remember. Now you come along, a damned half Indian, and you kiss her."

"Take it easy, kid. Ruth doesn't tell it that way."

"She did till you came along." Rusty threw his cigarette into the river. "You're different than anything she ever seen before. She'd have been satisfied to settle down with me in Lost Valley, but now she'll think of you as long as she lives. I ain't good enough for her now."

"A man doesn't deserve a woman he can't win," Horn said. "I don't reckon either you or me will tell her who to marry. She'll make up her own mind."

Rusty was silent a moment, a hand rubbing his chin. Then he said: "Well, she's got it made up. I can tell you that. And I'm telling you something else, mister. You'd better treat her right. Settle down and give her a home, or I'll . . . I'll. . . ." He stopped and took a long breath, then he asked: "Well, what are you going to do?"

"I don't know," Horn said. "I aimed to ride out of camp tonight, but Morgan asked me to stay another day till you got to the valley."

"You love her, don't you?" Rusty demanded.

Horn hesitated, knowing that loving her and marrying her were two different things. He said finally: "Yes, but I'm not sure I'll ask her to marry me. Like it's been said, I reckon I'm half Indian."

Rusty's hands fisted. "But you'll marry her just the same, and you'll take her away with you. You'll take her to hell-an'-gone, and she won't have nothing."

"What do you aim to do?"

Rusty kept rubbing his chin, staring at the river. "I don't know, but if I married her, I'd give her a home and I'd do all I could to make her happy."

"I want her to be happy," Horn said, "but there's one thing you haven't figured on. Suppose you lost your money?"

Rusty pinned searching eyes on Horn's face. "Why would I lose my money?"

"You've given it to Morgan, haven't you?"

"How did you know?"

"Ruth told me."

"She shouldn't have said. . . ." Rusty stopped. He picked up a rock, and threw it into the river. "Yeah, and I've been scared ever since we left home. Angus was what I'd call a failure in Ohio, but he's a good talker. When he's talking, you forget the things he ain't done. You just think about the things he says he's gonna do. Besides, I thought it was one way to make Ruth love me."

Ruth turned from the cook fire, calling: "Supper!"

"All right." Horn rose. "Rusty, we both love Ruth. If you're the one who can make her happy, I won't get in your way."

115

The boy got to his feet. Some of the antagonism had gone out of his face. "I can say the same to you." He cleared his throat. "Ruth says we need you. Not just for to-morrow but for a long time. You know the country, and I don't trust Ike Webb no further than I can throw my horse by the tail. Will you stay with us?"

Horn ran his boot toe through the gravel, staring down at the mark. This was the last thing he had expected from Rusty. He could curse the day he had signed on with the colony, but that wouldn't do any good. If he rode off, he would never forget he had left these people. They'd lose out and some would die, and it would be on his conscience.

Ruth had turned again from the fire. Seeing that they hadn't started toward the wagon, she called again, sharply this time: "Supper!"

"Coming!" Horn shouted.

He raised his eyes to Rusty's face. He saw the fear and the worry that were there. Rusty Hancock stood to lose both his money and his girl. It was enough to make any man worry.

"I ain't one to beg," Rusty said doggedly, "but I'm beg-ging now. For Ruth and me and all of us."

"I'd stay," Horn said at last, "if I knew I could help, but Morgan won't listen to me."

"We'll make him listen," Rusty said grimly. "There's more talk about him than you know. We're all worried."

"I'll think it over," Horn said, and swung toward the Morgan wagon.

When they came up, Ruth said with some asperity: "It took you a long time to get here."

"Big palaver," Horn said.

Webb usually ate with the Morgans, but he was not around tonight. Angus Morgan hunkered by a wagon wheel, eating with wolfish relish, ignoring Horn's presence. Night had settled down around them, the last color fading from the western horizon, and on both sides of them the ridges were lost to sight, merged into the blackness of the sky.

There was silence all around them, the weird, haunting silence of the wilderness. It was a thing to frighten people who were not used to it. Horn understood how it was with the colonists. They had come from a settled land, had rolled across empty plains where they could see for miles in any direction. The Rockies had slowly taken form before them, Pike's Peak raising its great, barren shoulders to the sky.

Now they were deep in the Shining Mountains, and the cañon walls pressed against them. Tomorrow they would see the valley that had been promised to them. Tonight the worries and fears that had been growing in them had suddenly become monstrous. Lost Valley might turn out to be a worthless desert or it might be the Promised Land that Angus Morgan had talked about in such glowing terms. They weren't sure, and so much depended on it.

Horn put down his empty coffee cup. "Where's the fiddler, Ruth?"

She had been leaning over the cook fire. Now she turned to him, her face flushed by the heat. "A couple of wagons from here. Why?"

"He'd better tune up. This camp feels like a funeral being born."

She shook her head. "He won't play, Jim. I asked him a while ago."

Morgan rose. His voice lacked its usual booming quality of certainty when he said: "Something's wrong. Ought to be dancing and singing, one day away from the end of the trip,

117

but they're sitting around like it was a wake."

"We'll stir 'em up, some way," Horn said.

He would have said more if he had not heard horses coming down Lost Creek. He rose, putting his tin plate and cup on the ground. He had expected this, but they were later than he had thought they would be. Morgan heard them then, and stood rigidly, his head cocked, listening.

Someone farther down the river yelled: "Indians!"

Another man bawled: "Get your rifles or we'll lose our hair!"

"No Indians around here, are there, Horn?" Morgan demanded.

"We wouldn't hear them if there were." Horn ran toward the men who had shouted, calling: "Leave your rifles in the wagons. These men aren't Indians."

He heard women cry out in relief, heard men curse in low voices, and one demanded: "Then who in hell would be riding in at night like this?"

"We'll find out. Come up to Morgan's wagon. If there is trouble, I'll handle it." Horn swung around. "Rusty, throw some wood on the fire."

Horn walked back, more worried than he would admit. He knew what panic could do. If the colonists got boogery and someone fired a shot, there would be hell to pay. Even as he strode toward the wagon, he heard a woman cry: "What are we doing in this God-forsaken country, Carl? Just try to tell me."

It was the Larsons. Carl Larson was one of the trustees of the colony, a carpenter by trade, but little different from the farmers and the rest, just a man with a family who had believed Angus Morgan. His voice came to Horn, quite calm: "God never forsakes a country where His people are. Let's remember that, Sadie."

118

His words stilled the worry that had risen in Horn. The little people were like that. Give them half a chance and they'd make out. They'd be afraid, they'd fuss and fume and wish they were back home, but when the chips were down, they'd come through if they had the right leadership. That was the trouble. Angus Morgan was not the right leader.

Horn came to Morgan's fire that had flamed up and was throwing a flickering light on Ruth and Rusty who stood between it and the wagon. Morgan had crawled into his wagon. When he came out, he carried a Winchester.

Horn said: "Put it back, Morgan."

Morgan squared his big shoulders, and his head jutted forward. "Don't give me orders, Horn. I'm thinking we made a mistake asking you to stay."

"That may be," Horn said, "but it was a bigger mistake when they elected you president of this colony."

"Do what he says, Dad," Ruth urged.

Rusty picked up the axe. "Put it back, Angus. Let's see how Horn handles this."

Morgan held the rifle on the ready, fighting his pride, black eyes alive with the desire to kill the man who defied him. Horn met his gaze, right hand wrapped around gun butt. He said: "Morgan, you're like a good-looking horse that you ride hard for fifty yards and then he caves. Put that Winchester back."

He broke as Horn had been sure he would. No bottom to him, no real talent for leadership. He had been a failure in Ohio, Rusty Hancock had said, and he'd be a failure here. Some men were like that, hoping a change of scenery would make heroes out of them, but it never did.

Morgan made a slow turn and slid the rifle into the wagon. Then he faced Horn, saying sullenly: "You'd better know what you're doing."

Horn said nothing. He eased his gun into leather and moved to stand by the fire, aware of the crowd that had gathered behind him. The incoming horses were still hidden by the darkness. Five or six of them, Horn judged.

He asked: "Where's Webb, Ruth?"

"I don't know," she answered. "I haven't seen him for an hour or more."

The riders came to the edge of the firelight, and one called out: "What outfit is this?"

Horn had expected to see Newt Kimmel and some of his Clawhammer crew, but these men were strangers to him. He answered: "The Ohio-Colorado colony."

"Where you headed?"

"Lost Valley."

The speaker swung out of the saddle, the rest remaining where they were. A tough lot, Horn saw, all but their leader packing guns on their hips and Winchesters in their scabbards. The one who had spoken reared back, hands in his pockets. He seemed different from the others—a dude, perhaps a gambler from Pueblo. He was wearing a ruffled silk shirt and a dove-colored broadcloth suit. Now he lifted his white Stetson and bowed to Ruth. His chestnut brown hair was slicked down, and, when he spoke, his voice was velvet smooth.

"You're a fair woman to find in such a wild country. You belong in Denver, not out here where your beautiful black hair will eventually adorn some Ute teepee."

Horn heard the girl catch her breath. He said hotly: "State your business, friend."

The dude brought his gaze to Horn. "A long hair, by the eternal. Do I have the pleasure of speaking with Wild Bill Hickok?"

"I'm Jim Horn. I guided this outfit from Fort Wallace."

"Why don't you cut your hair?"

"Why are you wearing them dude britches?"

The man laughed with his mouth but not with his eyes. He motioned to the others who stepped out of their saddles, one of them moving aside to stand by himself. A gunslinger, Horn saw, with two black-butted .44s carried low and thonged down. He was a slender, pale-eyed man, typical of those who made killing their business. The plan was plain to read. They had brought this man along to kill anyone who gave them trouble.

"Why, that's fair enough," the dude said, his voice still soft. "I'm Clay Vance, representing the Rocky Mountain Land Company. Who's the leader of this party?"

Morgan stepped forward, glowing with the importance of his position. He said: "I am. What can I do for you?"

Something was wrong here, terribly wrong, but at the moment Horn could not put his finger on it. Ike Webb was not in camp. Perhaps Morgan had told him about Rusty Hancock's money. That might be it. Or it might be something else. Horn had never heard of Clay Vance or the Rocky Mountain Land Company. If the company was big and legitimate, he would have heard of it.

Vance was silent for a moment, eyes sweeping the crowd and wagons. Then he stepped forward, right hand extended. "I'm pleased to meet you, Mister . . . ?"

"Morgan. Angus Morgan." He took Vance's hand, his sense of importance growing. "We left Ohio last fall with more than two hundred souls . . . men, women, and children. Everyone is a worker, Mister Vance. A few of the men are single, but most of them are family men. All of us have one thing in common. We expect to make our homes here and to grow with Colorado. We are a co-operative colony,

121

working together for the common good."

"A commendable undertaking, sir." Vance's eyes touched Ruth's face. "This is your daughter, I presume. I seem to see a resemblance."

"That's right," Morgan said indulgently. "I'm proud of her, and, as you can see, I have a right to be."

"What's your business, Vance?" Horn cut in.

Morgan wheeled on Horn, outraged. "Keep in your place, Horn. Whatever business our visitors have is with me."

"I said I'd handle the trouble," Horn said, "and that I aim to do."

"There is no trouble," Morgan said.

Horn gave him a thin grin. "You know, Morgan, a man can smell trouble if he has a nose for it, but you couldn't smell a skunk if he fired under your nose."

"You can't smell what isn't here, my friend," Vance said smoothly. "Now, Mister Morgan, I presume you have some capital."

Morgan nodded, swinging back to Vance. "Enough to get a start. We hope to be in Lost Valley tomorrow night. We will begin at once to clear the land and get in a crop. For a time we will live in tents. Houses can wait till fall, but crops cannot."

"Quite right, quite right. Now one more question. You have artisans as well as farmers, I suppose?"

"Certainly. As a matter of fact, we have brought a small sawmill with us that will be set up at once. We plan to erect a colony building that will house a store, an office, and a school room. We will not neglect the education of our children. We have a teacher with us, several carpenters, blacksmiths, and tinsmiths. We will also have a gristmill. You can see that we have no consumptives among us, no weaklings. Every member of our colony was carefully selected from the best people in Ohio."

"You've done a fine job, Mister Morgan," Vance said. "Your people are the kind we need in Colorado. As you doubtless know, statehood is not far ahead for us." He coughed apologetically. "But I am forced to give you bad news. You will not settle in Lost Valley."

Morgan's face went blank. Ruth cried out involuntarily, and someone in the crowd began to curse. It was Rusty Hancock who moved into the firelight, demanding: "What do you mean by that?"

Vance swung to one of the men behind him. "I'd like for you folks to meet Ben Travis. Tell them, Ben."

Travis, a burly man with a ragged beard, stepped up beside Vance. He took off his hat, raised a hand to his round head, and scratched it. "It's purty damned lucky for you folks that Clay Vance happened to be here, or we'd have come a-shooting. I represent the settlers of Lost Valley. There ain't no room for you. I'm right sorry, but that's the truth of it."

"Now hold on," Morgan fumed. "We sent a man to Colorado last summer before we left Ohio. He spent some time in Lost Valley looking it over, and he told us there were no settlers in the valley."

Travis laughed shortly. "We're there just the same, and we don't aim to let no greenhorns come in and push us out."

"But . . . but . . . there must be room for us," Morgan whispered.

"Room?" Travis laughed again. "Sure, if you want to go to the south end of the valley that's as dry as a bone. If that's what you want, come ahead, but you'll starve in a year. It'd take a goat to live down there."

There was silence for a moment, the kind of silence that comes when people are too stunned to speak. Horn did not look at them. He knew what he would see on their faces; he knew how they felt. He still did not understand the game these men were playing, but it would come out now.

Morgan wheeled to face Horn. "Why didn't you tell us about this?"

"You had faith in Webb," Horn murmured. "Remember?"

"Yeah," Rusty said harshly. "That's right, Angus. Horn tried to tell you, but you knew it all."

"It's been several years since I was in the valley," Horn said. "At that time there were no settlers there. Just a ranch, Newt Kimmel's Clawhammer. I figured, you might have trouble with him, but I didn't know about these yahoos."

"If you was there a year ago," Travis said in an ugly voice, "you'd know. . . ."

"I said *several* years ago," Horn cut in.

"All right, several years. Anyhow, you'd have seen us. You've been worked, Morgan, and it's my guess the long hair done it."

"I should have known!" Morgan shouted wildly. "He worked us for a fee. That's all, a guide fee, but he hasn't been paid, and he won't be."

"Dad, you're not being fair," Ruth cried. "If we've been deceived, it was Webb who did it."

"I said I had faith in Webb!" Morgan shouted in a great voice. "I still do."

"I guess you've gabbled enough." Horn nodded at Vance. "I suppose you're a farmer, too. You look like one."

Vance shook his head, smiling affably. "You're wrong, long hair. I happened to be in Pueblo when I heard about you folks. I came on ahead to stop trouble. Otherwise, as

Travis told you, they would have come shooting to protect their homes."

"We'll still do some shooting," Travis said truculently, "if you greenhorns think you're gonna settle in Lost Valley."

"These are reasonable people, Ben," Vance said quickly. "There need be no trouble. The instant I shook hands with Mister Morgan, I saw that he was both reasonable and intelligent. Now I have an alternative to offer, folks. My company owns a large grant of land some distance to the south. We'll be glad to have you settle there. That's why I asked the questions I did. I had to ascertain what sort of folks you were. You'll do, Mister Morgan."

"Where's your grant?" Horn demanded.

"I'm talking to. . . ."

"Where is it?" Horn asked again.

Vance licked his lips, his gaze flickering toward the gunman as if to be sure he was still there. Then he said: "It's on the Picketwire. You'll have to backtrack and swing south, Mister Morgan, but it will pay you. How much land do you expect to take?"

"Twenty thousand acres."

Vance nodded. "I see. Well, we have several choice blocks you may choose from, Mister Morgan. It's good land. Plenty of water. Fine timber. And there is one thing you may not have thought about. We'll sell the land to you and you will have titles at once. If you were to settle in Lost Valley, you would have to preëmpt or homestead because it is government land."

"Get on your horses and drift," Horn said.

"Now wait . . . ," Morgan began.

"Stay out of it, Angus," Rusty said in a hoarse voice. "This looks like a cheating shenanigan to me. Before we make any deals, I want a look at Lost Valley."

"Then you'll be looking at some hot lead," Travis bawled.

Vance gave Rusty a pitying look. "You're a boy, my friend. Just a boy. The value of age is that wisdom comes with it. I judge your people are willing to follow Mister Morgan's advice, or they would not have chosen him for their leader."

"Maybe we made a mistake." It was Carl Larson, standing well back in the crowd. "What's your idea on this, Horn?"

"I've got just one idea," Horn said. "Looks to me like Webb threw in with these yahoos to cheat you. Vance is lying as fast as a dog trots. I never heard of the Rocky Mountain Land Company, and I don't think there is any such outfit."

The gunman moved forward, right hand hovering over gun butt. "I'm a settler, long hair, and I don't cotton to being called any of the names you're giving us."

Horn's eyes swung quickly to Vance and Travis and the rest. He saw anticipation in their eyes, sensed the cool certainty that was in them. The gunman, whoever he was, had been hired as insurance against just such a situation as Vance was facing now. They must have known that Jim Horn was with the colony, and that brought Horn's thinking to Ike Webb.

"You're no settler, mister," Horn said evenly. "Get back under the rock you just crawled out. . . ."

The gunman made his draw, the fast sure movement of a man who lived by the gun, but still he was too slow to do the job. He had made the mistake of underestimating Jim Horn. Horn had his gun clear of leather before the other's Colt was leveled. He fired, the roar of the explosion rolling out into the quiet. The gunman's shot came like a belated echo, the slug kicking up dirt ten feet in front of him. He bent forward, a hand coming up, then he broke at knee and hip and spilled forward.

Horn swung his gun to cover Vance and his friends. He saw the shocked surprise that gripped them and heard Vance say: "You *are* Hickok."

"Pick him up." Horn motioned to the dead man. "Put him on a horse and git, the whole damned bunch of you."

They obeyed in sullen silence, and, when they had mounted, Vance put his hands on his saddle horn and leaned forward, eyes filled with wickedness. "I will tell you whoever tries to bring a wagon up Lost Creek will be shot." Then, with Vance leading, they rode away into the darkness.

For a long moment there was no talk from the colonists, no movement. Then Morgan said in a shocked voice: "You killed him."

"I reckon I did." Horn ejected the empty shell, and thumbed a new one into the cylinder. "You know what would have happened if I hadn't?"

"He'd have killed you," Rusty Hancock said.

Turning, Horn brought his gaze to Ruth's face. She stood as if paralyzed, her cheeks very pale. He thought bitterly: *Now* she *thinks I'm half Indian.*

"It was murder!" Morgan shouted, suddenly filled with righteous indignation. "We have a position in our constitution and bylaws to take care of. . . ."

Horn wheeled on him. "You are a greenhorn, Morgan, the greenest one I've ever seen. Don't you have any idea what I've done for you?"

"I have." Carl Larson pushed his way to the fire. "You risked your life when you could have played it safe. We're beholden to you, Horn."

"Beholden?" Morgan spluttered. "Why, Horn's tried to tell me how to run this colony from the day we left Fort Wallace."

"You need some telling," young Hancock said. "Looks like we're in a fix."

"We could have dickered with Vance!" Morgan shouted. "If we can't go to Lost Valley, we could have settled on his grant."

"No," Horn said. "He hasn't got a grant. There's some land on the Picketwire that can be bought, but it doesn't belong to any Rocky Mountain Land Company. Besides, if there is a grant company, it's probably having trouble. There'd be questions about any title they'd give you."

"We came to settle Lost Valley," Carl Larson said stubbornly. "Before I take the word of the men who were here, I aim to see the valley."

"And get ourselves shot . . . ," Morgan began.

"Maybe not. What we just saw proves to me that Jim Horn is a fighting man. If I ain't mistook, this calls for fighting. That right, Horn?"

"Looks like it," Horn said, "but if these men have actually settled the north end of the valley, you're in a tight and no mistake about it."

"We came all the way . . . !" a woman screamed.

"Wait!" Larson shouted. "Wait, now. There must be some way to handle this. How about it, Horn?"

Horn glanced at Morgan, sullen-faced and bitter with resentment. This had been his first real test, and he had failed miserably. There had been more talk than Horn had guessed, more suspicion of Morgan, more distrust of his leadership. "No sense of me saying anything," Horn said. "Morgan doesn't want my advice."

"*I'm* asking for advice," Larson snapped.

"But Morgan's president of the colony."

"I reckon the rest of us have some say about the way this colony is run," Larson said angrily. "Our constitution and bylaws provide for the president calling a meeting of the board of trustees when we run into an emergency, and I say this is an emergency."

"I'm not calling a meeting of the trustees." Morgan stood by the fire, facing the crowd, striving desperately to hold to his mantle of leadership. "I started this colony. It was my idea from the beginning. Time and time again it has been proved that a number of people, working together, can do things an individual cannot. The Greeley colony proves it. Jim Horn does not believe in the very principle we stand for, yet you ask him for advice."

Another man had moved up to stand beside Larson, a blacksmith named Fred Collins. Horn did not know him well, for he was a silent man who seemed capable of living within himself, but he had been respected enough by the colonists to have been elected a trustee. "It is time for plain speaking, Angus," Collins said. "I believe your words hypnotized us or we would never have left Ohio. We're here now, and we can't go back. I believe we can make a go of this undertaking if we do the right thing. If we make a mistake, we're defeated. It is time for a meeting of the trustees."

"We'll do the right thing!" Morgan cried. "I promise you we will, but at a time like this it would be foolish to listen to this man." He motioned to Horn. "He owns nothing but his horse and his saddle and his long hair."

They continued to stare at Morgan, their hostility a heavy pressure against him. Horn, watching them, sensed a dogged strength in them he had not felt before. What they had seen tonight had aroused in them something that had been dormant and had at last been awakened by this raw land. A few minutes before they had been afraid. Since then they had been threatened, they had seen a man die in the violent manner that had been typical of the West since the days of its birth. Their distrust for Angus Morgan had crystallized, their faith in Jim Horn had grown. They were watching Jim, waiting for him to speak, hopeful that he could point the way for them.

Still Horn hesitated, realizing more than ever the depth of his love for Ruth and knowing how Angus Morgan would feel toward him if he were responsible for the man's removal from office. It was Ruth who forced Horn's decision. She walked toward him from where she had been standing beside the back wheel of the wagon, her head high. She put her arm through Horn's and faced the crowd, her back to her father.

"I think this talk about Jim's long hair is crazy," she said. "Long hair didn't hurt Samson."

Angus Morgan was generous enough to laugh and say: "I hadn't thought of that. All right, Horn. Speak up."

"As I see this proposition," Horn said slowly, "there's just two things you can do. There's still good land to be bought along the Cache la Poudre and the Saint Vrain. From what I've heard, the Greeley folks are doing fine. The altitude is lower, and that makes the crop-growing season much longer."

"That's a long trip from here," Larson objected.

"And we'd have to buy the land," Collins added.

Horn nodded. "But it's railroad land, and you'll get a clear title. Or you can preëmpt government land."

"We'd be there too late for a crop this year," Larson said.

"That's right."

"How much would it cost?"

"Oh, maybe four dollars an acre."

Larson laughed shortly. "And we want twenty thousand acres."

"Which makes eighty thousand dollars," Morgan said maliciously. "Where are we going to get that kind of money?"

"What's the other thing we can do?" Rusty asked.

"Homestead in Lost Valley." Horn hesitated, not wanting to say what was on his mind. "Maybe we'd better sleep on it and decide in the morning just what we want to do."

"We won't do no sleeping the way we feel," Larson said. "We'll have that trustee meeting first thing in the morning. You hear, Angus?"

"What good do you think it will do?" Morgan asked harshly.

"Four heads are better than one," Collins said. "Strikes me we made a mistake sending out a one-man locating committee."

Horn nodded. "Webb's pulling out just before Vance and his bunch rode in doesn't look good."

"Ike Webb is all right!" Morgan bellowed. "I would trust. . . ."

"We've heard that too many times," Larson said angrily. "Don't say it again. Horn, I've got one question that I want answered before we go to bed. Can we make the grade in Lost Valley?"

"I think so, but you'll have to fight. I don't see any way out of it."

Larson nodded and turned away. "Let's go to bed."

Silently the crowd moved toward the wagons. Horn sensed the misery that was in them, the misery of people who have dreamed big dreams, and then have seen them fade. Now they must face brutal reality, but they were not shying away from it, as Angus Morgan had, and in that fact Horn saw some hope for them.

Horn remained by the dying fire, smoking, aware that Morgan had come to stand beside him. He did not look up, and presently Morgan said: "I hired you for a guide. Nothing more. Now you have stolen my daughter and you have destroyed the faith my people had in me. I believe that gives me ample reason to kill you, Horn."

Horn did not look up. "Answer a question for me, Morgan. If Webb had been to Lost Valley, why did you need a guide?"

"He didn't know the route a wagon train should take. He traveled horseback. We moved slowly, and we had to have grass and water."

"There might be another reason," Horn said.

"What?"

Horn gave him a direct stare. "I don't think Webb ever came west of Pueblo. It's my guess he met Vance there, and they cooked this up."

"You're crazy," Morgan snapped. "I've got everything staked on Ike Webb's honesty."

"That's one of your mistakes."

Morgan squatted beside Horn, and threw some wood on the fire. He said: "They'll try to vote me out of office to-morrow. Maybe it isn't important, but there's one thing that is."

"What?"

"Ruth's safety and her happiness."

Horn studied Morgan for a moment in the firelight. It was a different Angus Morgan now, more humble and with the swagger and the sense of self-importance drained out of him. Horn said: "She'll be all right."

"I wish I could be that sure." Morgan took a long breath. "I watched you kill that man tonight. It proved something I knew from the first. You're a savage, Horn. You wouldn't know how to treat a wife like Ruth."

"She'll make her choice."

"But it isn't a fair one. There's something about you that appeals to her. Your strength, perhaps. Or your talent for doing many things and doing them well. Or the ruthlessness that's a part of you. But whatever it is, I promise one thing. If you hurt Ruth, I'll kill you."

"You should *if* I hurt her."

Morgan rose. "We understand each other?"

"I understand you," Horn answered, "but you don't understand me."

"I think I do," Morgan said. "You can give the new president advice in the morning." Morgan went on to his wagon.

Horn let him go. Words would be wasted. Angus Morgan would never change, but Horn had learned one thing about the man that surprised him. He loved Ruth more than he did himself. Horn rolled another cigarette, and smoked it, wondering what Morgan would do if they removed him from office.

Morgan and Rusty Hancock slept under the wagon, Ruth inside. Usually Horn made his bed by the fire, but a restlessness was in him tonight that he did not fully understand. It was not that he really expected an attack. Clay Vance would take a more roundabout way to accomplish what he wanted.

Tomorrow, Horn thought, Vance would try again. Perhaps he would make another attempt to sell a bogus land grant to the colony. Or he might make an offer for Travis and the rest of the settlers to withdraw from the valley for a sum of money. That would be no solution. The colonists would not be able to pay what Vance would ask, and it would not settle anything with Newt Kimmel.

Horn rose and made a circle of the camp, telling himself that his fears had no real basis. If Vance meant to force a deal, he would not attack the camp. Trouble would come in the cañon, if the colonists tried to reach Lost Valley, and it would be real trouble. A handful of men with Winchesters, hidden in rocks on the sides of the cañon, could hold back the entire wagon train.

There was no sound now from the camp except the sonorous snoring of tired and worried men. Horn returned to the fire, thinking he should try to sleep. Tomorrow would be a rough day. Still, he could not throw off the sense of danger. He rolled another cigarette, and put more wood on the fire, and thought of Ruth.

The decision would be his, and it must be made soon. It might hurt Ruth, but in the end she would forget him and marry Rusty who would give her a good home. It would be all right. He kept telling himself that, but all the time he knew he was wrong. No matter how far he rode, he would never forget. He was the kind of man who took one woman into his heart; she possessed all of it, and there was no room for another.

Yet there was Ruth's happiness to think about. He had been called half Indian. Morgan had just said he was a savage. Well, maybe it was true. Half true, anyway. He was a drifter, a man who refused to live by what most people called normal standards. His long hair and buckskins were marks of his independence. But in reality they were more than that. They were throwbacks to a former era when life had been filled with the daily adventure of grappling with the primitive forces of the wilderness. To Jim Horn's way of thinking, society was false and dishonest, a point Ruth would never understand.

Today Ruth had left no doubt of her feelings for him. It was strange, because all the way from Fort Wallace she had seemed friendly but no more than that. Thinking about it now, he wondered if she had been as distant as he had thought. Perhaps, as she had said, it was a man's place to do the pursuing, and she had not let him know how she felt until they had reached the time when he planned to leave.

A faint sound from the darkness penetrated his consciousness. Probably some animal searching for food. He looked around and saw nothing to alarm him. He heard Morgan's heavy breathing, saw the vague mounds under the wagon that were Morgan and young Hancock. He turned back to the fire, wondering why he was so jittery.

It came again, more definite and closer, the swishing of a man bellying toward him through the grass. He whirled, right hand reaching for his gun, and realized at once he did not have time to get it out of holster. Ike Webb came lunging out of the darkness, the firelight glittering on the naked steel of a knife in his hand.

Chapter Two

Horn did the only thing he could, for there was no time to pull his gun from leather. He fell forward on his face, a maneuver totally unexpected by Webb. Horn felt the blade rip through his buckskin shirt. He humped up, threw Webb off, and scrambled to his feet.

There was time then to shoot the man, for Webb had fallen into the edge of the fire. He clawed frantically to get clear of the coals, cursing shrilly in pain, and in that instant a gunshot slammed into the night. Webb rolled over on his back and lay still, right hand flung out, the knife falling from lax fingers.

Rusty Hancock crawled out from under the wagon, a smoking gun in his hand. He shouted: "I got him, Horn! I got him dead center."

Horn restrained the fury that gripped him. A dead Ike Webb was not what he wanted. When he had dumped Webb into the hot coals, he had placed the fellow at his mercy. It had been his intention to beat the man until he talked. Now Webb had little time left for talking.

Horn dropped to his knees beside the stricken man, asking: "Why did you want to kill me, Webb?"

The camp had come to life. There were shouted questions, lanterns bobbed here and there among the wagons, and a baby started to cry. Morgan came to stand over Horn, and Ruth, pulling a maroon robe over her slender body, had slipped out of the wagon. Rusty Hancock stared at Webb, the jubilation gone out of him. His eyes were fixed on the blood that made a dark stain on Webb's shirt, and only then did he seem to realize that he had killed a man. Turning, he stumbled to the river and was sick.

"Did Horn shoot you, Ike?" Morgan demanded. "So help me, I'll hang him to the nearest tree."

Horn rose and hit Morgan, knocking him back against a wagon wheel. He said—"Stay there, damn you!"—and knelt beside Webb again. There was blood on the dying man's lips, small bright bubbles, and his face was gray. "You haven't got long, Webb," Horn pressed. "If you want to clear yourself in hell, you'd better talk."

"I'll be there ahead of you, Horn," Webb breathed, "and I'll blackball you. We'd have pulled this off if it hadn't been for you."

Others crowded up, Larson and Collins and some more. Ruth was there, and now Morgan began edging back, one hand feeling gingerly of his jaw.

"We've got a lot of women and kids in this outfit," Horn begged. "If they starve to death this winter, it'll be on your head."

Webb was going fast. His right hand was clutching his bloody shirt, his left clenched in agony. His eyes were glazed, the defiance gone now, and fear of the unknown was in him. He had enough life to whisper: "Me and Vance . . . were . . . going . . . to . . . split . . . the fifty . . . thousand. . . ." That was all. He shuddered, his right hand slid off his chest, and his mouth fell open. The vacant expression of death took possession of his face.

Horn rose and faced the crowd. "Rusty woke up in time

to see Webb try to knife me, and he let go with a shot." He could hear Rusty beside the river, and he held back the rest of the things he wanted to say. The boy had done what he thought he should, and there was no use in condemning him for it.

Larson stared down at the dead man. "I don't understand this, Horn. He said something about fifty thousand. You suppose he meant dollars?"

"He meant dollars, all right." Horn pinned his eyes on Morgan who stood in the inner circle of the crowd. "Wonder how Webb knew that much *dinero* was in the wagon train?"

"There ain't," Larson said in disgust. "We're as poor as Job's turkey. Somebody sure fooled him."

Morgan stared at Webb, shoulders slack. Watching him, Horn wondered what was in his mind. Stubborn as he was, and pinning his faith in Webb as he had, Morgan could no longer doubt Webb's guilt.

"Better go to bed," Horn said. "We'll plant him in the morning."

They faded away into the darkness, muttering questions that could not be answered. The frightened baby whimpered, then it was silent, soothed back to sleep by the mother's soft singing. Horn, watching Morgan's grim face, wondered if the man was touched by those sounds, whether he even heard them.

Ruth stood alone, a slender dark shadow close to the wagon. Horn said: "Get some canvas, Ruth. We'll wrap Webb in it."

She brought the canvas, and Horn rolled the body in it and carried it away from the fringe of firelight. When he came back, Morgan and Ruth were standing beside the fire. It had died down until it made only a dull glow in the darkness. Horn could not see Ruth's face clearly, but he felt the tension that lay between the girl and her father, and he came to her and put an arm around her.

"Get some sleep," he said. "You'll need it tomorrow."

She shivered, pressing close to him as if seeking strength from him. She asked: "There'll be more trouble?"

"A lot more," he said. "I can't figure any way out of it."

"Dad told Webb about the money, didn't he?" Ruth asked tonelessly. "And Webb had sold out to Vance?"

"That's about it," Horn answered. "I figured Rusty had just a dab, but fifty thousand is worth a heap of killing. Vance aims to have it."

"Go to bed, Ruth," Morgan said in a low, bitter voice. "I have something to say to Horn."

"There's nothing you can say now," Ruth whispered. She walked to the wagon, and crept inside.

Horn threw more wood on the fire as Rusty came around the wagon, stepping over the tongue slowly as if he lacked the strength to go around it. He dropped to the ground beside the fire, his face very pale.

"I killed him, Horn," Rusty said. "I saw him and the knife, and I just shot."

Horn knew the boy still did not realize the extent of the mistake he had made, and he could not find the words to tell him. He said: "It's all right, Rusty."

"But I killed a man," Rusty breathed. "You shot that fellow tonight and you didn't turn a hair. It was just like killing a prairie dog to you."

"Webb needed killing. So did the man I drilled, but don't ever plug the wrong man or it'll be on your soul as long as you live."

Rusty looked at Horn in the fire light, sweat making a shine on his bony face. He said: "Yeah, I guess Webb deserved it all right. What does it mean, Jim?"

"It means you're fetching a hell of a lot of *dinero* into a country like this," Horn said bluntly. "Morgan should have known better."

"We need money to develop a new country," Morgan said harshly. "Don't condemn me, Horn."

"Condemn you?" Horn gave a short laugh. "I don't need to. You've done it yourself. Most fellows do a few good things to balance off the mistakes, but all you've written down in the book are mistakes."

Morgan's fists knotted, and he took a step toward Horn. Lacking the courage to do what he wanted to do, he stopped, and wiped a hand across his face. He breathed: "I've tried to do good for a lot of people, and I will if you let me alone."

"I don't aim to let you alone. Yesterday I was ready to take my pay and drift, but now I'm staying."

"If it's Ruth you're staying for," Morgan said in a low voice, "I'll tell you once more you can't have her. I'll kill you first."

Morgan would try. Meeting the man's eyes, Horn was sure of it. Morgan would never forgive him for knocking him down. Sometime he would make his try, if he had the opportunity, perhaps in the darkness or from the protection of brush or timber, or a boulder big enough to hide him. Angus Morgan did not have the courage that it took to fight in the open, but he was all the more dangerous because this was so. And he was Ruth's father.

"Maybe it's Ruth," Horn said. "Or Rusty's money that he deserves to keep. Or maybe it was the baby I heard crying a while ago. Did you ever think what winters are like in this country, Morgan, with hungry kids?"

"It was cold in Ohio," Morgan said, "and kids got

hungry there. Out here they've got a chance to get their bellies full."

"A mighty slim one. I reckon that's why I'm gonna hang and rattle." Horn motioned wearily. "Now go to bed before I beat hell out of you."

Morgan wheeled back to his bed under the wagon.

Rusty said: "I'll sit up, Jim. If I try to sleep, I won't see anything but Webb, lying there with my bullet in him."

"Think of it this way," Horn said. "There never was a place in the West that was gentled down without some killings. That's our job. We've got to gentle down Lost Valley so these women and kids can live there and be safe."

Rusty nodded eagerly. "I want a hand in it, Jim." He took a long breath. "I've hated you from the day we left Fort Wallace because you've taken Ruth away from me. You didn't know it, but I did. Well, it's like you said this evening. If a man can't win a woman, he don't deserve her. I found out something else, too. I just ain't man enough for her."

Horn rolled a cigarette and was silent, his eyes on the flames. He wanted to think of Ruth and his love for her, of her kiss and the way she had clung to him, but the picture would not come clear. Angus Morgan was in the way. A man could not kill the father of the girl he loved—but he could be killed by him.

They sat there that way until the camp stirred to life with the first drab light of dawn. The wood was gone. Horn took an axe and, with Rusty trudging beside him, moved upstream to a dead cottonwood and began chopping. He was bone-tired when he drove the axe into the limb, then the weariness dropped away from him. This was something to do, something physical that for the moment took his mind off Angus Morgan, and he felt the better for it.

Horn cut more wood than Ruth needed for breakfast. Other men were chopping around them, and he motioned for some of the boys to help themselves to the wood he had cut.

Presently Larson moved over to him, asking: "What are your plans, Horn?"

"I'm going into the valley right after the burial."

"You'll need help." Larson sleeved sweat from his face. "I didn't sleep none after the shooting. Kept thinking about the money Webb said was here. Must be in the wagon train or it wouldn't be working like this. You know, Vance riding in last night and wanting to sell us land on the Picketwire."

Horn chopped a limb in two and, straightening, leaned on his axe. He asked: "Larson, how well did you know Morgan before you left Ohio?"

"Not real well. He had a newspaper in a town about fifty miles from where Sadie and me lived. Times were bad and I was out of work. Morgan came around, signing folks up for this colony, and, well, we'd heard about the Greeley colony. Morgan made it sound good. He's right persuasive, you know. Uses big words real handy."

Horn nodded, knowing how it had been. Larson was like the rest of them, little men reaching for the rainbow that Morgan painted for them. The hell of it was that Morgan really wanted to help. It was probable that he honestly hoped to take young Hancock's money and double it for him, out here where money was scarce and opportunities were waiting like ripe plums to be picked from a tree.

"Better have breakfast," Horn said. "We've got a job of burying to do."

It was Horn and Rusty and Collins who dug the grave close to the base of the hill. It was Larson who made the

142

marker and carved Webb's name on it. They gathered around the grave, all the colonists, including the children, and Morgan read from the Bible. Then, lifting his face to the morning sky, he prayed. He knew big words, Horn thought, and he used them well. If Horn needed proof of Morgan's talents, he had it here in this simple service.

They lowered the body into the grave, and the people moved back to their wagons, all but the men who remained behind to fill the grave. Morgan walked across the grassy flat to Collins, saying: "We'll have the meeting now." He looked at Horn, hating him with his eyes. "You want to sit in on the meeting?"

"No. I ain't a member of your colony."

"I had the impression that you thought you were," Morgan said evenly.

"Then you're making another mistake," Horn said, and swung away toward his horse.

Horn saddled his black gelding and rode to the river. He loosened the cinch, and stood there while his horse drank, unaware that Larson had come to stand behind him until the man said: "What do you hope to accomplish in this valley?"

Turning, Horn looked at the man's broad grave face. He said: "I ain't sure, but I want to see if Travis and his bunch really have settled the valley."

"Is it safe for us to try going up the cañon?"

"Hell, no. They'll pick you off like sitting ducks on a pond." He tightened the cinch. "I rode for a fellow named Newt Kimmel who used to have the only ranch in the valley. Newt came here when the Utes were thicker'n flies, and he stuck it out. Claimed the whole damned valley. I figured he'd be the one who'd give you trouble."

"You think he might help us?"

Horn shrugged. "Newt is no hand to help any batch of sodbusters, but there's something fishy about this deal. It isn't like him to let Travis and this outfit settle the valley."

Larson scratched his nose, the corners of his mouth jerking. He said: "Horn, I'm scared worse'n the day I got married, but this is our fight a lot more'n it's yours. I'll go along."

"Thanks, but I'll do better by myself."

Relieved, Larson nodded. "Well, we ain't got a pretty job on our hands, voting Morgan out of office."

"There's one thing you've got to make 'em savvy." Horn stepped into the saddle. "You folks came from a country where you could call a sheriff or a policeman when you got into trouble. Out here there is no law except what you make with your Winchesters."

"I'll get it through their heads," Larson promised, "if I have to pound it in with a hammer."

Horn rode upstream, keeping his eyes straight ahead. He did not want to talk to Ruth this morning. She might get it into her head to go with him. He splashed across Lost Creek, spread thin here in the gravel beside the river, and fifty yards farther west began angling up the steep south wall of the cañon.

It was slow going through the cedars, and Horn made frequent stops to blow his gelding. An hour after he left the river, he found a deer trail and by mid-morning had reached the top. Lost Valley lay before him. For a long moment he sat his saddle, thinking again, as he had thought many times when he had ridden for Newt Kimmel, that if he had to settle down in one place for the rest of his life, he would pick Lost Valley over any other spot he had ever seen.

To the west the Sangre de Cristo range raised gaunt

granite peaks thousands of feet above the floor of the valley. Here and there patches of snow remained, defying the sun. Far to the southeast he could see the Spanish Peaks, made hazy by distance. Pike's Peak was visible to the northeast. Directly to his left were the ragged, pine-covered foothills of a lower range, and there, he knew, was fine grama grass and range as good as a man would find anywhere.

Lost Valley was a cowman's paradise. He could not blame Newt Kimmel for marking it as his own. Kimmel had held it against other cattlemen and against settlers. It seemed unreasonable that Ben Travis and his bunch could have successfully defied Kimmel. They would not have remained a week when Horn had ridden for Clawhammer.

Horn turned his gelding southwest. From here he could not see the Clawhammer buildings, but they were not far from him. He would reach them by noon, and he would know the answer to the question that had been plaguing him since Clay Vance and the others had ridden into camp the night before.

Lost Valley was too big and too good for one man to hold indefinitely, a fact of which Kimmel had long been aware, but he'd told Horn many times that he'd hang on as long as he could. Meanwhile, he'd be homesteading the best part of the valley. His headquarters were on the north fork of the creek, a low, well-watered section of the valley carpeted with blue joint and wild timothy that furnished good winter graze. During the summers his cattle were driven up into the spruce and aspens on the shoulders of the Sangre de Cristo range or into the pines to the east.

Newt Kimmel had never been one to consider death. Or if he had, there was his daughter Dixie to think of, a red-headed tomboy that Horn had been certain would never grow up. He remembered her as a fiery-tempered kid with pigtails down her back and a brain that could think up more deviltry than any boy Horn had ever known. She would be eighteen now, and Newt close to fifty. It was hard to picture Dixie that old, and even harder to think of Newt being middle-aged, but time never stood still. There would come a day when Jim Horn would be middle-aged. He wondered sourly if he would still be wearing buckskins and long hair just to prove that he had not surrendered to an encroaching civilization that had already brought steel rails to Denver and plows that were turning the sod of thousands of acres along the Cache la Poudre and the St. Vrain.

Silly! Just plain damned silly, one man standing against a powerful current. He could hate this thing people called progress, but he couldn't hold it back any more than Newt Kimmel could keep his grip on Lost Valley. Jim Horn was outmoded; he might as well get a haircut and admit it. They would come, the farmers and the blacksmiths and the carpenters, the Carl Larsons and the Fred Collinses and the Rusty Hancocks. Yes, and the Angus Morgans and the Ike Webbs and the Clay Vances. The solid men and the riff-raff.

If Horn had been as true to his principle as he had thought, he would never have guided the colony from Fort Wallace. But there had been a woman. In the beginning, he had not thought of it that way, but he was honest with himself now. He loved Ruth Morgan, loved her enough to forsake his principle of giving no help to those who brought what they called civilization. If he had held unalterably to that principle, he would have gone on and let Vance and Travis rob the colonists, let Morgan fail as a man with his conceit was bound to fail.

Horn came into an open spot atop a ridge and reined up.

He looked down upon the Clawhammer buildings, but he saw them only with his eyes. Something had become clear to him that had never been really clear before, even though he thought it had. He had reached the point at last where he must surrender. Ruth Morgan meant that much to him. He thought of Rusty Hancock's money and the good that could be done with it here in the valley. He thought of the child he had heard crying during the night and its mother's lullaby. They were wrong when they had called him half Indian and a savage. If he had been, he would have ridden on as he had planned. There had been a day when a man could control his life, but that day was gone. He had been blind or he would have seen it a long time ago. He had not wanted to see it. That was the whole truth of it.

He lifted his reins to ride on when he heard a shout. He hipped around in his saddle, right hand reaching for his gun. Then it fell away, and he swore softly. Ruth and young Hancock were riding up the ridge, Ruth waving to him. Then they were out of sight in the scrub oak, and he sat there, waiting, a cold rage growing in him. The thing he had wanted more than anything else was to keep Ruth out of danger.

It was another fifteen minutes before they emerged from the brush and rode up beside him, Rusty's face bleeding from where a limb had slashed him, Ruth's blouse torn under her left arm.

"Don't get mad," Ruth said the instant she could be heard. "You had no right to ride off without saying anything to us."

You had no right! He stared at the girl, weariness from the hard ride showing in her face, then he looked at Rusty who was dabbing at the cut on his cheek. A moment before

Horn had been telling himself he had reached the point where he would surrender. Now rebellion rose in him. It was a hell of a thing when a man couldn't ride out of camp without being followed and told what he didn't have the right to do.

"Yeah," Rusty said. "Damn it, Jim, you can't take all the risks. It's our fight more'n it's yours."

"You shouldn't have brought Ruth," Horn said hotly. "I don't know what I'm headed into."

"But you wouldn't have headed into it if it hadn't been for me," Ruth said. "You'd have gone on and you'd have been safe by now. Don't you see?"

"Go on back."

She shook her head, lips tightly pressed. "No."

Rusty shifted uneasily in his saddle. "It ain't that we're just tag-alongs, Jim. Ruth said she had to come, and I couldn't let her come alone."

"You left your money . . . ?"

"Nobody in the colony will steal it. Seemed like the thing for me to do was to give you a hand."

He looked at the girl, and then at Rusty. They thought they were right. They thought they could help him. He could not bring himself to tell them they'd be in the way, that whatever he had to do he could do better by himself.

"Come on, then," Horn said brusquely. "I'm going to the ranch yonder. Won't be any trouble there, I reckon."

He rode down the slope, Ruth on one side of him, Rusty on the other. They reached the creek that curled slowly between willow-lined banks, crossed it, and came up to the south side, horses straining in the mud before they achieved solid footing.

"I think it's magnificent," Ruth said in a low voice. "It's the most beautiful valley I've ever seen."

"Clay Vance thinks so, too," Horn said, his voice still brusque.

"A man could raise grain here," Rusty said. "Don't seem so dry. Plenty of water to irrigate with if we have to, and there's timber for our sawmill. Looks good to me."

Good if they could fight and hold it, Horn thought, but he killed the temptation to put it into words. Instead, he said— "Short growing season."—and let it go at that.

Ten minutes later they reached the Clawhammer buildings. There was no change here, Horn thought. The same sprawling log house shaded by ancient cottonwoods, the barns and outbuildings, the pole corrals. It was as if he had left only yesterday.

"You know, Jim," Rusty said, "I always had a notion I wanted to be a cowboy. What's the chance of getting a job here?"

Horn did not answer. Ruth was looking at the mountains, at the fresh pale green of the aspens and the black fingers of spruce that reached high up on the steep slopes, then she tipped her head back to stare at the gray granite that lay above timberline. She said reverently: "Jim, I guess every human being dreams of finding God's country. I believe we have."

Horn said nothing to that. He had more important things to consider than Rusty's wanting to be a cowboy or Ruth's finding God's country. Something was wrong here. The ranch seemed deserted except for the horses in the corral and the thin pillar of smoke rising from the chimney. Ordinarily there was a good deal of activity around the ranch. Now there was no sound to indicate human presence. He wasn't sure, for he had seen Vance's and Travis's horses at night and at some distance from the firelight, but he had a feeling that the bay and the roan geldings in the corral belonged to Vance and Travis.

"We've got trouble," Horn said in a low tone. "Rusty, pull your gun and leave it in front of you. Don't get squeamish if you have to kill another man."

Rusty hesitated, eyes whipping to the house and coming back to Horn's grim face. He asked: "What's wrong?"

"Dunno, but aim to find out." Horn stepped down, catching the blur of someone's face behind a window in the ranch house. He called: "Hello, the house!"

The front door slammed open, and a girl ran down the path, red hair streaming behind her. "Jim! Jim Horn!" It was Dixie Kimmel, grown up and almost as tall as Ruth. When Horn had seen her last, she had been a child.

Dixie kissed Horn and hugged him with the fervency of a woman who has just had a prayer answered. Then she brought her mouth close to his ear, her arms still around him. She whispered: "Don't come in." She drew back and looked at him.

He put a finger against her pug nose, grinning at her. "You turned out to be quite a woman. I never thought you'd make it."

She stepped farther away. "And I thought you'd have a haircut the next time I saw you. Still playing mountain man?"

"Naw. Aren't enough mountains no more. Just can't afford to go to a barber. I've taken to playing guide for a wagon train." He motioned to Ruth. "Dixie, this is Ruth Morgan. She belongs to the train, and she thinks this here valley is heaven. Ruth, this is Dixie Kimmel. Her dad owns Clawhammer."

"How do you do," Ruth said, her voice cool.

"Sure glad to know you, ma'am," Dixie said, "only Dad

doesn't own much of anything these days. And you're plumb wrong about this valley being heaven. It's a chunk transplanted from hell."

"She was just a kid when I rode for her dad," Horn said. "As ornery a brat as I'd ever seen. Dixie, the long drink of water yonder that didn't get the Lord to dye his hair as red as yours is Rusty Haycock. Says he wants to be a cowboy."

Rusty lifted his hat. "Pleased to know you, Miss Kimmel."

"Howdy," Dixie said. "I'm right sorry, but we aren't taking on any hands right now."

"Who's in there?" Horn asked.

Dixie bit her lower lip, frowning. Then she said: "A couple of no-goods named Clay Vance and Ben Travis. They're killers, Jim. Get back on your horse and ride off like you'd just dropped by to say howdy."

"Vance?" Ruth whispered. "Travis? What does it mean, Jim?"

"I'm wondering," Horn said. "Newt alive?"

"Yes, but that's about all. Go on now, Jim. Ride off, or there'll be hell to pay."

"Why, now," Horn said softly, "it just happens we have something to settle with those *hombres*. Rusty, don't go off half-cocked, but keep that iron of yours handy."

"Jim, you can't . . . ," Dixie began.

"Got to," Horn said, and, stepping past the girl, walked through a patch of shade to the house. He shouted: "Vance, you still got that grant on the Picketwire?"

Vance stepped through the door to the porch, as dudish and immaculate as he had been the night before. He put a hand on a porch post, smiling with cool confidence. "That I have, bucko. Change your mind about taking it?"

"It's worth talking about. Where's Travis?"

"In the house. Why?"

"I want to see him."

Vance tipped back his white Stetson and scratched his head. "Your business is with me, friend, if you want to settle on the grant."

"I've got a question to ask Travis. Call him out."

"What question?"

"I had an idea after the ruckus last night. Your outfit didn't look like farmers to me, so I got the notion that maybe you and Travis heard we were coming and saw a chance to sell something."

Vance unbuttoned his coat, exposing a short-barreled gun in a shoulder holster. He looked past Horn at Ruth, smiling amiably. "You're riding in bad company, Miss Morgan."

Ruth rode toward the house, worried eyes touching Horn's face briefly and swinging back to Vance's. She said: "It could be worse."

Vance laughed. "I don't take that kindly. I like beautiful women, Miss Morgan, especially if they have spirit. You know, women are like horses. If a woman is like a plow horse, she's no fun. No fun at all."

Horn made a half turn so that he could watch Vance and still see Rusty and Dixie who remained on the other side of the cottonwoods. He motioned for Rusty to ride up, knowing that Travis was inside and that he probably had a gun in his hand.

Jim Horn had been in some tight spots, but none as tight as this. There was a chance to play it through, but it was not a good chance, for it depended on Rusty Hancock. If the boy blew up too soon, Jim Horn was a dead man.

"I don't take kindly to being compared to a horse, Mister Vance," Ruth said coolly.

152

Vance laughed again, softly, with the confidence of a man who is sure of himself. "I'd call it a compliment, miss. It depends on the horse, of course, and the woman. I never ran into a horse I couldn't ride, or a woman I couldn't tame."

"You won't tame me," Ruth said, her chin thrust forward defiantly, "if that's what you're getting at."

"I'll take that bet," Vance said, "and give you odds. I'm a right good hand with women, and with your dad running that bunch of greenhorns I hold good cards."

"Damn you!" Rusty shouted.

"All right," Horn cut in. "Call Travis out, Vance. We've had enough palaver."

Irritated, Vance said: "I'm talking to the lady, long hair. She'll make a deal with me, and her dad will take it. I'll give odds on that, too."

"Then you'll lose your bet," Ruth said. "When we left camp this morning, the trustees were having a meeting. By now my father has been voted out of office."

Vance frowned, and his gaze shuttled back to Horn. "That right?"

"I think so," Horn said. "Morgan's made too many mistakes. Webb was one of them. Now are you gonna call Travis out?"

"What kind of offer do you figure to make Travis?" Vance asked.

"I had a notion he'd pull out for a price . . . with his friends."

"They might at that. Ben, come out here."

Travis appeared, a Colt in his hand. He stood there, a blocky man almost as wide as the doorway. He said: "I don't like the smell of things, Clay. We ain't heard from Ike."

"You won't either," Horn said. "You had it fixed for him to cut me up like a Christmas turkey, didn't you?"

"That was the idea," Travis agreed.

"I killed him," Rusty called out. "I've got you covered, Travis. Drop your gun."

Vance stiffened, his eyes swinging to Rusty as if this was a twist in the game he had not expected. Horn did not turn. His right hand was close to his gun butt. He said: "Vance, I'm guessing you're right handy with that iron you're toting. Now if you feel lucky, try your luck."

Vance shook his head. "I had my stack bet on Webb, and I saw what happened last night. I'm holding a good hand without taking any chances on dying."

"You're looking at the bright side of this," Horn said. "The kid's a good shot. He plugged Webb in the brisket."

"It doesn't matter," Vance said. "My boys are in the cañon. Anybody who tries to get a wagon into the valley is a dead pigeon. You'll settle nothing here."

"I'll settle Travis if he don't drop that gun!" Rusty shouted. "I'm scared. I'm so damned scared my finger's getting tight on the trigger."

Vance said: "Drop your iron, Ben. He might do it."

Travis let his gun go, cursing. "I told you I didn't like the smell of this."

Horn, watching the big man, made up his mind. Vance was the smart one, Travis the bully. Without Travis, Vance could be handled. Horn did not know how much depth there was to Ben Travis, but there was a good chance that, if he was badly beaten, he could be bluffed into leaving the country. At the moment it seemed the only way to play it.

"I reckon you put Webb up to knifing me, Travis," Horn said evenly. "Come down off that porch. I aim to beat hell out of you."

For a moment Ben Travis didn't move. His shoulders hunched up until his ball of a head was indrawn like a frightened turtle's, but Travis wasn't frightened. His tiny eyes, deeply recessed in their sockets, showed surprise, and then they began to glow with anticipation. A moment before he had thought the gun in Rusty's hand was enough to beat him, but now a new hope throbbed in him.

Behind Horn, Dixie cried: "Don't do it, Jim. He'll beat you to death."

Travis stepped down from the porch, walking slowly, great arms at his sides.

Horn said: "Watch Vance, Rusty. Keep him out of this."

Dixie cried out again, her voice panicky: "Don't do it, Jim. Nobody has licked Travis since he's been here."

"He's getting a licking now," Horn said.

It was Horn's guess that Travis was an expert at barroom fighting, the kind where no rules held. He'd butt with his head, he'd knee a man, he'd ram his thumbs into a man's eyes if he got him down. But Horn had done his share of that kind of fighting. He could take care of himself if Vance was kept off his back. That was his one worry as he moved in, driving his first blow into Travis's hard-muscled body.

Travis took the blow without so much as a grunt and lunged forward, trying to get his hands on Horn. Reach was on Horn's side, bull strength on Travis's. So Horn was faster than the big man, but knowing, too, that one mistake would be a fatal one.

The ground was uneven and deep with dust. If Horn stumbled, it would be the break Travis was counting on. For a time Horn fought carefully, keeping out of Travis's reach, slashing him across the face and hitting him in the chest, continually moving, while the dust stirred and rose around them.

There was no sound from the watchers. Vance smiled slightly as if there could only be one way for this to end. Rusty, his nerves as taut as overly tight fiddle strings, kept his eyes on Vance. Ruth was bending forward over the saddle horn, her face pale. Dixie was clenching her fists and swinging them with each blow Horn landed, her whispered—"Give it to him, Jim. Damn him, give it to him."— not even reaching Ruth's ears.

There was only one way to fight Travis: until the man was worn down, or irritated to the point where he left himself wide open. Horn held rigidly to that plan, slashing out with lightning fists, rolling his head and making Travis miss by a fraction of an inch when he threw a punch, or taking it on his elbows or a shoulder. All the time he was giving Travis brutal punishment. He chopped a right to Travis's nose and brought a stream of blood; he drove a left to the man's chest, a right to the eye. Between flurries he backed away until he had become familiar with every inch of the ground underfoot.

"Stand still and fight," Travis panted. "Damn your yellow hide."

Horn taunted him with a laugh. "You're hittin' nothing but air, mister." Coming in close, he rocked Travis's head with a vicious right.

Horn's plan was paying off. Not so much in the slow wearing down of Travis's great strength, for most of Horn's blows were slashing rapier thrusts that did little more than sting or cut. If it kept going this way, Travis would outlast him, for Horn had spent a sleepless night and was beginning to feel the slowing down that came from bone-deep weariness. But he was making Travis frantic in the way a mosquito does that bites and gets clear from a man's slapping hand to return and bite again. Sooner or later Travis would give way to fury.

Horn's opportunity came sooner than he expected. Travis threw a swinging right that started at his heels. It missed and threw him off balance, and Horn drove in and knocked him down. Travis fell face forward into the dust. He came up at once, coughing and spitting and cursing, and dived headlong at Horn.

Horn stood there, refusing to give ground, and brought his knee up squarely into Travis's face. The blow was perfectly timed. The *crack* of it was like that of a descending butcher's cleaver slamming into a side of beef. Travis's head snapped back on his short neck. Horn stepped aside as he fell.

This time Travis was slower to get to his feet. His wide face was a mask of sweat and blood and mud. He shook his great head as if the ability to think had been knocked out of him. There was a chance he was faking, but it was a risk Horn had to take.

Now Horn moved in fast. He brought his right through to the side of Travis's head, his full weight behind it. Travis's knees buckled, and his hands came down as he fought to hold himself upright. As he began to sag, Horn hit him once more with a powerful fist flush to the point of his bearded chin. This time Travis lay still when he fell.

Horn stumbled to the porch and sat down, wiping his face with his hands. He said: "Thanks, Rusty. I was afraid you'd take your eyes off Vance long enough to let him get his gun out."

"I watched him all right," Rusty said shakily, "and I was kind of hoping he'd go for his gun. Seems like our trouble would be over if he was dead."

Dixie had come to the porch, trembling a little. She breathed: "You should have killed him. You ought to kill

Vance. You ought to hang both of them."

"I'm hoping this will do the job." Horn motioned to Vance. "Saddle up. Take Travis and get out of the valley."

Vance laughed softly. "Well, my friend, you're tougher than Ike Webb allowed you were, but you haven't done the job. We have legally filed on our homesteads, and we will stay."

"I killed one of your men last night," Horn said, "and you've just seen what I've done to Travis. You're too smart a gambler to play your hand out."

"We'll see," Vance said. "We'll see."

Travis was getting up, still dazed, blood drooling down his face from a dozen cuts. Vance moved past him to the corral.

Horn said: "Go with 'em, Rusty. Keep 'em covered till they ride out."

Horn sat there, wiping sweat from his face until the other two had saddled and mounted. Then Vance called— "Don't make the mistake of thinking we're finished, Horn!"—and rode off, Travis behind him, swaying drunkenly in his saddle.

"I may have busted my hands up," Horn said. "Got some hot water, Dixie?"

"Sure have." Dixie looked at Ruth. "Come in, Miss Morgan."

"Take care of our horses, Rusty," Horn said, and followed Dixie into the house.

Ruth stepped down, giving her reins to Rusty who had ridden up, and went inside. Horn sat down at the kitchen table and began soaking his hands in a pan of hot water that Dixie brought to him. He looked at Ruth, grinning wryly.

"Sorry you had to see that, Ruth."

"I don't understand." Ruth dropped into a chair across

the table from Horn. "You forced that fight, Jim. Why?"

"I can tell you why he did," Dixie broke in as if irritated. "There's some folks you can argue with, but there's others you've just got to knock some sense into their heads. Jim was working on the same notion that Travis did when his bunch came to the valley. Travis opened up a saloon in his cabin. Our boys got to going down there, and Travis picked fights with a couple of them. Almost killed them. Soon as they could ride, they drew their time."

Horn flexed his hands, rubbed them, and put them back into the hot water. "Travis wouldn't pull a gun on me, Ruth. Using my fists was the best I could do. I'm hoping he'll pull out now."

"Might work," Dixie said. "He's been almighty proud of his fighting, so maybe he'll tuck his tail and run now that he's lost his reputation. Or he may hang around and try to dry-gulch you."

"What's been going on hereabouts?" Horn asked.

"Trouble!" the girl cried. "Nothing but trouble for the last six months. Vance's bunch settled on the creek. Vance offered to buy us out, about ten cents on the dollar. Dad laughed in his face. Then somebody dry-gulched Dad. Got him in the chest and he almost died. You won't know him, Jim. He just doesn't look the same."

"Can he talk?"

She nodded. "We've had the doctor from Canon City. He left some stuff to give Dad so he sleeps most of the time, but when he wakes up, he can talk your leg off."

Horn lifted his hands from the water, clenched them and opened them several times, and nodded as if satisfied. "Didn't hurt 'em none, I reckon." He walked to the stove and took a towel down from a nail on the wall. "What about your crew, Dixie?"

"What crew?" she demanded. "We don't have one. Chuck, Marty, and Jake were dry-gulched. Two more were beaten up like I told you. The rest took their time and left the country. We haven't had a man on the ranch for a month."

Understanding how the girl felt, Horn nodded. Newt Kimmel had never kept as big a crew as he should have. He'd always said there was no sense wasting money on cowhands' wages when there wasn't another spread within fifty miles, so he had depended on a few good men who had been with him for years. They were the ones who had been dry-gulched, and the rest, drifters who would not give their outfit the loyalty a good rider does, had sloped out of the country.

"What about your cattle?" Horn asked.

"I've done what I could," she said miserably, "but it wasn't nearly enough. They're scattered from one end of the valley to the other. We've lost some. I can't prove it, but I'm dead sure Vance's bunch has rustled several hundred and sold them in the mining camps where nobody cares what brand a beef's got on it." She turned away. "We're busted, Jim. Busted flat. I tried to get to Pueblo to hire a crew, but Vance won't let me out of the valley."

"Maybe some of our men could help," Ruth said.

Dixie whirled on her, saying: "How much good would a . . . ?"

"How about dinner," Horn broke in.

Dixie turned back to the stove. "I'll get it, Jim."

"Newt asleep?"

Dixie nodded. "It'll be evening before he wakes up."

"What was Vance doing here today?"

"More of the same. Trying to get me to sell. Dad would sell the place if I said so."

Ruth got up to help Dixie, and Horn walked into the living room. For a time he stood in front of the stone fireplace, massaging his hands and thinking that this room had not changed in appearance since the first time he had seen it. The crude furniture that Newt Kimmel had made when he'd settled in the valley, the guns on the walls, the bear rugs, the battered melodeon that had been freighted in from Denver—it was all as he remembered it.

It was essentially a man's room. Some women would have changed it, but Dixie had left it the way Newt liked it. Perhaps she didn't know how to change it, for she had been raised in a world of men. Her mother, Horn recalled, had died the first year they had been here.

Rusty came in, looking at Horn with new respect. He said: "That was sure a hell of a fight, Jim. You cut him down like he was a pine tree."

"Maybe wasted," Horn said bitterly. "I didn't know how the land lay, or I'd have done it different. I should have killed both of 'em like Dixie said."

Dixie called—"Dinner!"—and they went into the kitchen. They ate in silence, Horn's mind on Clay Vance. It was plain enough what the man was after. He wanted the gold that was in the wagon train, but that was incidental. His main object was to get Clawhammer. That explained why he didn't want the colonists in the valley. They might help Newt Kimmel, and that was the one thing Vance could not allow, not when he was this close to getting what he wanted.

When Horn finished, he pushed back his plate, and rolled a smoke. He said: "I want to talk to Newt. Maybe Ruth's idea wasn't so bad, Dixie. After we trim Vance down a little, I think we can work out a deal so Newt won't kick about the greenhorns coming into the valley."

161

"He's not in shape to make any kind of deal," Dixie said dully, "but you can talk to him this evening when he wakes up."

Horn rose. "I think I'll hike back to the river. Ruth and Rusty will stay here."

"What are you going to do?"

He grinned at her. "Well, now, I ain't just sure. I'll see how the voting went."

"I'm going back with you," Ruth said.

"No, you won't. You're done sashaying around over the valley. You're staying right here if I have to hog-tie you."

She frowned, fighting an impulse to argue with him. Then she said meekly enough: "All right, Jim."

"I'll fetch Collins and Larson back with me so they can have a powwow with Newt."

"Jim." Ruth had gone rigid, her eyes on the window. "Larson's coming."

Wheeling, Horn ran out of the house, Rusty behind him. Larson was riding up the creek as fast as he could make his jaded horse travel.

Dixie cried: "Look at that fool! He's killing his horse."

Horn ran across the yard and past the cottonwoods, knowing that something was wrong or the man wouldn't be riding that way. Larson reined up, his face grim.

"There's hell to pay," Larson said through dry lips. "Morgan talked better'n I thought he could."

Horn reached up and gripped his arm. "What happened? Damn it, talk."

"They kept Morgan in as president, and he persuaded them to try coming up the cañon. He's driving the first wagon."

Ruth cried: "He'll be killed! He will be, won't he, Jim?"

There were many things Jim Horn could have said about

162

Angus Morgan. This was defeat, the very move Clay Vance wanted the colonists to make. Once driven back down the cañon, they would not try again.

Horn thought then with a sense of guilt that he should have foreseen this. He knew the depth of Morgan's stubborn pride and he knew how well the man talked. But he said none of the things he wanted to say. There was no use hurting Ruth now. She would be hurt enough later on.

"I reckon he will," Horn said, "unless we can fetch him a miracle. Let's saddle up, Rusty."

Chapter Three

It took valuable minutes to rope a Clawhammer horse and change Larson's saddle to it, and to throw gear on Horn's and Rusty's horses. Horn carried a Winchester in his scabbard, but Larson and Rusty had only their belt guns. Horn reined up in front of the house and asked for rifles. Dixie brought them at once with several boxes of shells.

"Dad always said there wasn't any sense to putting money in a bank," Dixie said. "He claimed the best investment a man could make was in guns and ammunition."

She handed the .30-30s to Rusty and Larson. Horn's eyes turned instinctively to Ruth, standing on the porch in the trim, proud way she had, her shoulders back, her head high. She was able to give Horn a small smile and wave to him. It seemed to Horn in that short moment, when he tried to fill his eyes with the sight of her, that he had never loved her as much as he did now.

"Don't you worry, Ruth," Rusty said. "They'll be all morning getting harnessed up. We'll probably get to the cañon ahead of them."

It wasn't true, and Ruth knew it. She said—"Good luck."—and Horn, watching her, sensed that it was all she could say without losing her self-control.

The three of them rode down the creek, Horn turning

164

once to look back. He raised a hand to Ruth, then they made a turn, and the house was lost to sight behind a screen of willows. It occurred to Horn, as it had so often, that only a freak of nature could have made it possible for Angus Morgan to have sired a girl like Ruth. But freak of nature or not, she was his daughter, and she loved him.

Larson glanced at Horn, his face grim as if expecting Horn's fury to fall upon him. Finally he burst out: "I couldn't stop 'em, Jim. Damn it, I tried, but I ain't a talker like Morgan. It wasn't just the trustees. Morgan was too smart for that. He said this was for everybody to decide, so he called in all the men. He made a speech, and they went down the line for him."

"I thought everybody was against him," Horn said.

"Hell, they was, but I tell you Morgan's got a tongue. Should have gone into politics. He allowed we'd never see you again. Said you didn't have a nickel invested in the colony and you wasn't the kind to settle down with 'em, so you wouldn't give a damn what happened."

"Why, the crazy . . . ," Rusty began.

"I know, I know," Larson broke in, "but we wasn't sure you and Ruth would find him. Morgan's big argument was that every day counted. He said we had to get crops in if we wanted to eat next winter. When you get right down to brass tacks, I guess that was what's been worrying everybody more'n anything else."

"It's too late now," Horn said. "Won't be easy breaking sod up here."

"They didn't know that," Larson said. "What they wanted was a look at the valley. Morgan said if it didn't pan out good, they'd have a talk with Vance about his grant on the Picketwire. Morgan figured that Vance was bluffing about not letting anybody come up the cañon. He convinced 'em mighty quick when he said he'd take the first wagon. The women and kids are walking behind so they won't get hurt."

"That's more sense than I thought he had," Rusty muttered. "The hell of it is my money's in his wagon."

"We'll get it back for you," Horn said.

Rusty grinned. "I think you will, Jim. Damned if I don't think you can do anything."

"You could have stopped 'em if you'd been there," Larson said, "but I couldn't. When Morgan starts talking in that way of his, folks forget what they said about him yesterday, and they won't remember till it's too late."

"If it wasn't for Ruth," Rusty said bitterly, "I'd hope Angus gets it between the eyes. It's like I told you, Jim, I lived beside him, and I knew he was big talk and little do, but I came along just the same."

"How'd you find us, Carl?" Horn asked.

"Luck mostly. I seen the way you started. Followed your tracks long as I could. I lost 'em, but, when I got to the top of that ridge yonder, I saw the ranch and figured it was the best bet."

Horn nodded. There was no more talk for a time, and presently they reached the junction of the two forks of the creek. At this point the stream turned north, dropping quickly into the cañon. There was a cabin here, and Horn could see several more up the south fork, small log buildings with dirt roofs. There was no sign of life around them, no gardens or chickens or pigs, no ground broken by the plow. It proved what Horn had been sure of. Clay Vance and his bunch had never intended to stay and farm.

"Where do you reckon Vance and Travis went?" Rusty asked.

"Hard to tell," Horn answered.

"You figure they're around somewhere?"

Horn shrugged. "They might be drawing a bead on us now. Depends on how Travis took his beating. Vance may have trouble making him stay in the country."

They heard the first shots then, directly north and not far down the cañon. Horn wheeled his horse at once, nodding to the others, and rode along the west rim, keeping above the cañon that broke off sharply below them. The creek was a shining silver ribbon at the bottom, the road beside it little more than a boulder-strewn trail.

"Better get down there, hadn't we?" Rusty shouted.

Horn shook his head, calling back: "No! We've got to stay above 'em."

Ten minutes later they saw the first wagon. Morgan's, Horn guessed. It was lying on its side at the edge of the creek, both horses dead. Morgan would be somewhere around. He was probably dead, too, although he may have had strength enough to crawl into the brush. Stubborn to the point of being foolish, and bound to have his way, there could be no denying the peculiar kind of courage that had been in the man. He had not been able to face Jim Horn with a gun in his hand, but he had boldly flouted Clay Vance's order by bringing his wagon on ahead of the others.

Horn reined up in a thicket of scrub oak and, pulling his Winchester from its scabbard, stepped down. He had heard spasmodic firing from Vance's men, but he doubted that any more damage had been done. He judged they were throwing lead to warn the colonists more than anything else.

The cañon made a bend directly below Morgan's wagon, and from where he stood on the rim Horn could not see any of the others. Apparently Morgan had come some distance ahead of the second wagon, and the rest had stopped before they had come into rifle range.

Rusty and Larson had dismounted.

Horn said: "We'll tie here. They won't be looking for us to buy into the fight."

"Angus is a goner," Larson muttered, "or I'm mistook."

"Keep low," Horn warned. "We don't want 'em to spot us. We've got to get the rest of the wagons up before dark, or it'll be a hell of a bad deal."

Rusty said something under his breath. A man halfway down the cañon had fired a shot. He was directly below them, his head and shoulders visible. Rusty brought his Winchester to his shoulder, and, when Horn batted the barrel aside, saying—"No."—Rusty wheeled, fury boiling through him. "What the hell," he breathed. "It'd be like shooting fish in a barrel."

"It's a little more than that," Horn said. "Just how brave are you, kid?"

The fury died. Rusty sleeved sweat from his face. He said: "I ain't brave at all, Jim. Why?"

"I'm working on a notion. I think we can get those wagons up." The firing had stopped, and except for the one man below them there was no sign of life on either side of the cañon. Horn scratched his cheek thoughtfully. "You see, there isn't room for the wagons to turn around, and they can't back down. We've got to get 'em up."

"I don't see how," Larson said. "Hell, these devils can sit there all day."

"They know where your money is, Rusty," Horn said. "Chances are Morgan told Webb, and Webb told Vance. Come dark, they'll move down and take Morgan's wagon apart."

"And we sit here and watch them do it," Rusty said tonelessly.

168

Horn shook his head. "Not if you want to be bullet bait. Soon as another wagon shows up, they'll start shooting. If Larson can spot 'em, he can make it damned hot for 'em."

"Where you gonna be?" Larson asked.

"Busy."

"Bullet bait." Rusty shook his head. "Don't sound like fun, but I'll do it."

Horn grinned. "You'll do it, kid. Tell the rest to string along behind you. Won't take you more'n half an hour to get down there to 'em."

"It wasn't like this in Ohio," Rusty said. "Tell Ruth I. . . ."

"You'll be around to tell her yourself. Take it on foot and keep under cover."

"I don't like it," Larson said. "I'll go, Jim."

"You've got a wife and kids. Don't drive from the seat, Rusty. Walk on the right side of the team and stay close to 'em. First shot you hear, get under the wagon."

Rusty said—"I'll sure do that."—and started into the cañon.

Horn waited until the boy had disappeared, then he turned to Larson. "Stay here. If I'm doing this wrong, you'll have to shoot straight, or they'll nail Rusty."

"What are you up . . . ?" Larson began.

But Horn had already slipped down the slope, moving swiftly and quietly through the brush, careful not to start a rock rolling down the steep slope. He could still see the man that Rusty had started to draw a bead on. The fellow was lying motionless behind a boulder, attention on the turn in the cañon.

Horn did not know how many men Vance had, but it was a reasonable guess that the six he had brought into camp the night before was all of them. Collier was dead. It was not likely that Vance and Travis would be here. That left three, and, judging from the amount of firing Horn had heard when it started, that number would be about right.

It took fifteen minutes of careful maneuvering to reach a point above the rifleman. Here a sandstone ledge ten feet high ran along the side of the cañon parallel with the rim. A number of boulders lay along the edge with, here and there, a few runty cedars that gave scant cover. For most of the fifteen minutes Horn had been unable to see the man. If he changed position, Horn's plan would fail. If one of the others spotted Horn, he'd be a dead man and his plan would certainly fail.

Reaching the ledge, Horn bellied across it, entirely in the open now and visible to anyone above him. His spine began to prickle. He should have told Larson to shoot any of Vance's men who showed themselves above him, but it was too late now.

He eared back the hammer of the Winchester as he eased between two boulders. The man below heard the *click* and whirled as Horn's head appeared over the ledge.

"Stand pat," Horn ordered.

"The long hair," the man breathed. "You damned sneaking Injun."

"I think I'll lift your scalp," Horn said. "Your yaller hair will look good in my teepee."

Sweat beads popped through the skin of the man's face. He wet his lips, staring at Horn as if expecting a bullet any minute. Horn remained silent, letting fear work through the fellow.

"Go ahead," the man breathed. "Why don't you shoot me?"

"I decided I'd lift your scalp while you're still alive,"

Horn said as if he had given it careful thought. "Then I'll let you go. When Vance and Travis get a look at your noggin, they'll tear out of the country like bats out of hell."

The last bit of restraint left the man. He began to beg, his hands clasped in front of him.

Horn laughed contemptuously. He said: "You sure look comical. Where'd Vance find anything like you? What's your name?"

The man's flabby lips sagged open. He whispered: "It's D-Dyer. What do you want?"

"How many men are in the cañon?"

"Three."

"Where?"

"There's two of us on this side. One on the other."

Horn swore softly. That made it bad. He had hoped all of them would be on this side and that his prisoner could call them in. He asked: "How far away is the one on this side?"

"Right below me."

"Can he hear you?"

The man nodded.

Horn said: "Call him up."

"Suppose he don't come?"

"Why, I reckon I'll have me a yaller-haired scalp."

"I'll try." The man gulped and repeated: "I'll try."

"First thing you'll do is drop your gun belt over yonder with the Winchester. I'm not coming down to have a look-see, but if you've got a hide-out on you and you make a try for it, I'll blow your brains out."

The man unbuckled his gun belt with trembling fingers and tossed it toward the Winchester. Then he shouted: "Meeker! Come up here, Meeker."

The man below called: "What'n hell do you want?"

"They're sending some men up the cañon. Can you see 'em from where you are?"

"No."

"Then get up here with me. Looks like a hell of a lot of 'em. Regular damned army."

"What's the matter with your eyes?"

"Nothing. I'll need help picking 'em off, that's all."

Grumbling, Meeker clambered up the rocky slope and presently appeared through the brush a few feet from Dyer. He growled: "I don't like the smell of this a little bit. Vance and Travis ought to be here. If them greenhorns start to rush us. . . ." Then he saw Horn and stopped, mouth dropping open.

"That's fine, Meeker," Horn said. "Keep coming. Lay your Winchester and your gun belt with Dyer's on the rock."

The man obeyed, cursing Dyer in a bitter voice.

Dyer said defiantly: "He was gonna lift my hair. I couldn't do nothing. How'd I know he'd Injun up on me?"

"Didn't help none to pull me into it!" Meeker shouted angrily.

"What about Morgan in the lead wagon?" Horn asked.

"I got him with my first shot," Dyer said. "He fell out of the seat and crawled back into the brush. Ain't seen him since."

"Where's your third man?"

Meeker motioned across the cañon. "Over yonder. He couldn't hear us if we hollered at him."

"Then we'll go after him," Horn said. "Were I you, I wouldn't try to warn him or make a run for it."

To Horn's right the ledge broke off in a rock-strewn slant. Horn drew back and slid down it. There was a moment when either Dyer or Meeker could have safely made a dive for one of his guns or jumped into the brush and got clear, but their backs were to Horn and they didn't have the opportunity until it was too late.

Horn, two steps behind them now, said: "Head for the creek."

They made a slow descent, both Meeker and Dyer being careful not to give Horn an excuse to shoot. They reached the road beside the creek, and Horn, uncertain whether the man on the east side of the cañon could see him or not, stepped behind a cottonwood.

"Now it's up to you boys to fetch your partner down here," Horn said.

Meeker and Dyer swung to face him. Dyer started to whine, and Meeker cuffed him across the side of the head with an open palm, saying: "Shut up. That ain't gonna get you nothing with this *hombre*."

"That's right," Horn said. "I'm running out of time and patience."

"Damn it," Meeker said bitterly, "we can't do what we can't do. Benson's too high up to holler at."

Horn had not realized how nearly the time he had given Rusty had run out. Now he heard the *clatter* of a wagon and his eyes turned downstream, quick fear knifing through him as he realized his scheme was not working, and that he was likely to be the cause of young Hancock's death.

Horn saw the wagon, and in that same instant the man above him cut loose with his Winchester. Meeker, taking advantage of Horn's shift of attention, grabbed for a gun in a shoulder holster. Horn had a glimpse of Rusty, diving under the wagon. Then he heard the report of a .30-30 high up on the western rim and knew that Carl Larson had located the man across the cañon.

Everything seemed to happen at once, too many things

173

for Horn to grasp at the moment, but he caught the motion of Meeker's hand as he went for his gun and barely had time to swing his rifle from Dyer to Meeker and fire. Meeker stumbled forward and fell. He rolled over once into the creek, and lay still.

Dyer started to run downstream toward Rusty's wagon.

Horn yelled: "Hold it!"

Dyer, panicky now, began to zigzag in a frantic effort to escape. Horn let go with a shot that kicked up gravel at his feet. Rusty, still under the wagon, cut loose with a shot that caught Dyer in the neck. He went down in a headlong fall, and Horn, running behind him and coming up to him, saw that he was dead.

Rusty scrambled out from under the wagon, and began to talk to his horse and pull on the lines. Horn dropped his rifle, and took hold of the bridles, helping Rusty quiet the horses, aware that he was making a fair target for the man on the cliff above him. Both Larson and Vance's man had stopped firing, but that might not mean anything. As soon as the team quieted down, Horn moved back beside Rusty.

"I killed another man," Rusty said bleakly. "I keep trying to remember what you said. About men like these needing killing."

"You're saving the county hanging money." Horn put a hand on the boy's shoulder. "A man wouldn't want a better partner, kid. I was plenty worried there for a minute that I'd got you into something."

"Hell, you were into something, wasn't you?"

Horn shrugged. "I'm used to it. What kind of a shot is Larson with a Winchester?"

"He's a good shot. We all did some hunting back home. I guess we wouldn't stack up with you when it comes to pulling a six-gun, but when we've got time to aim, any of us would do pretty good."

Horn looked up at the brushy east side of the cañon. "Wish I knew about that *hombre* up there. Just the three of 'em, and we sure as hell fixed these two. Funny thing what a man will do when he gets boogery. That Dyer fellow never should have run. No sense to it."

There was silence for a moment. Horn was still studying the east side of the cañon, when a faint voice called: "Horn! You out there, Horn?"

"Morgan," Rusty whispered. "He's over yonder. In the brush."

Wagons were coming upstream now, and Horn was still not sure about the man above him. He hesitated, knowing that he could not reach Morgan without coming into view of the rifleman above him, but he judged that Morgan had been hard hit or he would not have called like that. Horn lunged toward him, bending low, and dived into the brush, expecting a shot that did not come. He bellied toward the wounded man, keeping a screen of willows between him and the road.

Morgan lay on his back, eyes closed, a dark bloodstain on his shirt. His face was pale, so pale that for a moment Horn thought he was dead. He crawled forward until he was beside Morgan, and felt of his wrist.

"I'm alive," Morgan whispered, "but I won't be long. Where's Ruth?"

"She's at Clawhammer. She's safe."

"Keep her safe, Horn. I'm giving her life into your hands. I would not have done that a few hours ago. I had planned to kill you."

Morgan's eyes were still closed. His pulse had been a faint throb, so faint that Horn had had trouble finding it. Horn sat motionless, saying nothing. He could not think of anything to say to a man who had hated him as Angus Morgan had, and who now was dying.

"I've had time to think about a lot of things," Morgan went on. "I knew I was a goner and there was no one to help me. I wanted to talk to Ruth, but it's all right, now that I know she's safe. Tell her I love her, Horn. Just tell her that."

"I'll tell her."

"Queer how a man's values change when he gets to the place I am. I've been a failure, Horn. You seemed to know that the instant you signed on with us. I'm a failure whose only talent was with words. I trusted Webb, and I thought I had to go on trusting him no matter what you said."

Morgan was silent, and Horn thought he was gone. Then he opened his eyes and tried to see Horn. Failing, he closed them again. He breathed: "The light's out. Won't be long, so I've got to hurry. I'm going to ask something of you. I never thought I would. Stay with the colony, Horn. They need you. Will you promise me that?"

Jim Horn possessed his share of weakness. He had made his mistakes and he'd had his failures, but he had never gone back on his word. If he gave it now to a dying man, it would be doubly sacred. He hesitated, hating this man who, waiting at the portals of death, wanted to bind his future.

"Perhaps someday you will understand how it has been with me," Morgan whispered, "always striving for something I could not attain. First it was for my wife, and then for Ruth. Now you've got to do what I wasn't big enough to do. Promise me, Horn."

Dry-lipped, Horn said: "I'll do what I can."

A moment later Morgan was dead. Horn rose, and stood looking down at him, wishing he could have known Ruth's mother.

When Horn got back to Rusty's wagon, two others had come up behind it and stopped. Fred Collins, walking upstream toward Rusty, saw Horn and called: "Is it safe to move up now?"

"I think so," Horn said. "There's one yahoo up yonder I'm not sure about. I'll go see to him." He motioned to the brush where Morgan lay. "You'll have to elect a new president."

Rusty and Collins were silent for a time, both looking away from Horn as if they felt they should say they were sorry and could not bring themselves to do it. Then Collins muttered: "Too bad for Ruth."

"Yeah, she's gonna take it pretty hard." Rusty pinned his eyes on Horn. "She's sure gonna need you now."

"I'll be around," Horn said.

Picking up his rifle, Horn waded across the creek. Larson, almost down the west slope, called: "I got that fellow up there, Horn! Spotted him as soon as he cut loose at Rusty."

Horn swung up the slope, angling to the south. He wanted to be alone as much as anything. He thought of the promise he had made Angus Morgan and wondered if he could do anything for these people. It depended on several things—and on Ruth, on the colonists, and on their chance of success. Too, there was his own future to consider.

There was this pulling and hauling within him, his love for Ruth on one hand, and on the other his fear that it would be wrong for him to marry her. As Rusty had said, he'd take her "to hell-an'-gone and she won't have nothing." He knew himself, knew his inherent sense of rebellion against authority and the accepted standards of a settled life. So, because he loved her, he was afraid to marry her. He wondered if other men found only misery in a matter that should make them happy.

He found the body of the man Larson had shot and turned back down the cañon. He reached an open space, and stopped on a sandstone ledge to smoke a cigarette, idly watching the men below him as they righted Morgan's wagon. They brought another team up, and Rusty climbed into the seat.

Wagons rolled up the cañon, dust boiling around them. Women trudged along the road. Kids played in the creek, chasing each other and slipping on wet rocks and tumbling in to get soaked head to foot. A moment before there had been danger. Now it was over, and the children had forgotten it. It was too bad, Horn thought, that a grown person had lost so much of the ability to forget.

There was nothing for Horn to do until camp was made and a meeting called. Clay Vance, he knew, could not be counted out. Men like Collier and the three who had been killed today could be hired by the dozen in Denver or Pueblo or Trinidad. Vance had been too close to success to quit now. He might leave the valley, but he would be back. Besides, there was Ben Travis.

Horn went down to the creek and crossed it, stepping between two wagons. He nodded at the driver of the one below him and climbed the west slope. Rusty's and Larson's horses were still here. Horn untied them, mounted his gelding, and, leading the other two, rode south along the rim until he reached the head of the cañon. Rusty, he saw, was bringing Morgan's wagon up the last steep pitch. The others were strung out behind him as far as Horn could see down the cañon, a weaving line of weathered canvas tops.

"Jim."

It was Ruth's voice. Horn hipped around in his saddle,

178

surprised to see Ruth and Dixie coming toward him from the cabin at the forks. He saw the question in Ruth's eyes, and looked away. He would have to tell her. She came on toward him, and, when he brought his eyes to her again, he was surprised to see the composure in her face.

"He's gone, isn't he?" Ruth asked in a low tone.

Horn nodded. "I was with him when he died. He said to tell you he loved you."

She bowed her head, fighting to hold her calmness of spirit. Horn waited, sitting motionless in the saddle, wanting to comfort her, to help her through these hard moments, but not knowing what to say or do.

Ruth raised her head to look across the valley at the towering Sangre de Cristo range. "We'll bury him here, Jim. No matter what happens to the rest of us, he'll be here forever. That would be a victory for him, wouldn't it, Jim?"

"Yes," he answered. "He died a brave man, Ruth. He took the lead wagon and kept the others behind him so they could stop before they got into rifle range. That's why no one else was hurt."

"A brave man," Ruth said softly. "He would like to know you had called him that."

Then Jim Horn knew he could not hate the memory of the man who had bound him with a promise. Angus Morgan had had his weaknesses, but he had had his strengths, too, and they had been easy to overlook. The colony would never have reached Lost Valley if it had not been for him.

"We'll camp here tonight." Horn motioned toward the grassy flat that lay between the forks of the creek. "We'll have a palaver after supper."

"Have you seen Vance or Travis?" Dixie asked.

Horn shook his head. "We got the three that were in the

cañon. Two of 'em were called Dyer and Meeker."

"I know them," Dixie said. "The third one was Benson, but they're just small fry. Nobody's safe as long as Vance is alive."

"Newt?"

"Still asleep when I left. He'll be waking up about dark."

"You staying here?"

Dixie glanced at Ruth who was walking slowly toward the Morgan wagon that had reached the top and was rolling on toward the flat between the forks. "For a while, Jim. She can't keep that stiff upper lip forever." Dixie gave Horn a searching look. "She's got more to her than any greenhorn woman I ever saw. She's your kind."

"I ain't sure I'm hers," Horn said. He was silent for a moment, watching the wagons roll over the crest, and grinned when a man yelled: "Hooray for Lost Valley!" Horn swung his gelding toward the wagon behind Rusty, calling back: "I'll tell Larson to keep an eye on things! I'll get Rusty, and we'll go have a talk with Newt."

"I wish you would," Dixie said. "I don't like leaving him alone."

Larson had taken the wagon that Rusty had been driving, and, as Horn rode toward it, he heard Rusty tell Ruth: "Both of your horses were shot. We had to pull another wagon over to the side and put the team on yours."

"Dad?"

"He's inside. Don't look at him. Won't do no good."

Horn was out of earshot then and reining up beside Larson who was leaning forward in the seat, a wide grin on his lips. "Well sir, we kind of fixed Mister Vance's boys, now, didn't we?"

"But Mister Vance isn't fixed."

Larson scratched his head, the grin dying on his lips.

"No he ain't. Well, I see you brought our horses up. You must have done more walking today than you've done for a spell."

"Reckon I have. Carl, I've got a notion that this is the time to settle what you folks are gonna do. Rusty's got about all the *dinero* that's in the train, hasn't he?"

Larson nodded. "Fact is, he's got all of it. I didn't know he had it till Webb let it out. Morgan must have aimed to use it to get us started, and I guess Rusty figured on letting him."

"Before Morgan died," Horn said, "he made me promise to stay with the colony."

"Well, now, that's good. Dunno what we'd have done without you."

"That promise holds till you're on your feet, and I've got an idea for putting you there. Rusty and I are taking a ride. You run things while we're gone. Roll the wagons into a circle and put guards out. Watch the stock. You'll be in a hell of a fix if Vance runs off your horses."

"We'll do it," Larson promised.

Horn rode on to the Morgan wagon, leading Rusty's horse. Ruth was still standing there. Rusty had stepped down from the seat and was talking to her. When Horn rode up, the boy turned to him.

"She wants to bury him here," Rusty said.

Horn nodded, thinking that in time there would be a town here called Morgan City and Angus Morgan would become a legend, his failings forgotten, his virtues magnified. He glanced down at Ruth who was still holding her composure, and he thought it would be better if she let herself go and cry.

"Dixie's gonna stay with Ruth," Horn said. "Rusty, I figured you and I would ride back to Clawhammer."

"All right," Rusty said, puzzled.

"Don't go sashaying around, Ruth," Horn said.

She nodded, but said nothing. Horn glanced up at the sun that was low over the mountains, jerking his head toward Clawhammer, but Rusty still hesitated. He put a hand out to Ruth and dropped it as if uncertain what to say.

"Go on," Ruth whispered. "I'm all right. Dying isn't so bad, you know. I mean, that's the way we have to look at it. It's just that Mother went a long time ago, and I haven't had anybody but Dad for so long."

"You have me and Jim . . . ," Rusty began.

"Of course, I have," she said quickly. "Go on with Jim, Rusty. Hurry before I start to cry."

Horn touched the brim of his Stetson and reined away. A moment later Rusty came up beside him, saying: "I guess there's nothing that makes a man feel as worthless as having someone you love lose someone she loves. I can't feel real sorry about Angus, but Ruth. . . ."

"She'll be all right," Horn broke in. "I don't know about things like that, neither, but Morgan showed more guts dying than he ever did living. I've got the notion that if you and I do what we've got to do, the colony will be all right, and that'll please Ruth because I'm guessing this colony was the biggest thing her dad ever tried."

"What have we got to do?" Rusty asked.

"First I want to know if you've really got that fifty thousand in the Morgan wagon?"

Rusty nodded. "In gold. It's in a false bottom that I rigged up myself."

"How'd you come to have that much *dinero?*"

Rusty scowled. "Hell, that ain't none of your business."

"It isn't for a fact, but if I take you to talk to Newt

Kimmel, I aim to find out if there's any strings attached to that *dinero*."

"No, it's mine. My dad was pretty well fixed. Had a store and some other property. After he died, Morgan talked me into turning everything I had into cash and coming along. I told you I figured Ruth. . . ."

"I remember," Horn said impatiently, "but there's some other things I don't know. Morgan aimed for you to invest in the valley, didn't he?"

"Yeah, he wanted to build a town out here and I was supposed to be the banker. Loan my money till everybody got on his feet. We've got a gristmill and a blacksmith. . . ."

"I know all that. Now I'm gonna put it up to you. If you don't give these people some help before winter, they'll be starving by spring. You still want to invest in the valley?"

"I dunno," Rusty said gloomily. "I've lost Ruth, but I ain't begrudging it. I mean, after seeing what you've done." He shook his head. "It's kind of hard to say, but you and Ruth go together like sugar and cream. If you'll settle down. . . ."

"Damn it, we aren't talking about me and Ruth. Before we get to Clawhammer, I want to settle one thing. What are you gonna do with that fifty thousand?"

Rusty was silent a moment, his eyes on the Sangre de Cristo range, granite peaks set against the scarlet sky like giant saw teeth. He looked south at the valley with its green grass and willows along the creeks and, then hipping around in the saddle, looked back at the eastern hills touched with the sharp light of the dying sun. He came around slowly, a hand raised to rub his bony face.

"It's a pretty valley," he said. "I've got a hunch our people will make out. I'll see it through, Jim."

"That's fine," Horn said. "I reckon you'll be that banker

Morgan was talking about."

They rode in silence until they reached Clawhammer. The sun was down by the time they dismounted. "I'll see if Newt's awake yet," Horn said, and went into the house. A moment later he returned. "We may have to sit a while. Newt didn't look like he'd ever wake up. He's lost fifty pounds since I last saw him."

They watered and fed their horses, and went into the house, Rusty lingering in the doorway until Horn had lighted a lamp. Horn carried it into Kimmel's bedroom, motioning for Rusty to follow. The Clawhammer owner lay in bed, a single quilt pulled over him. For a moment Horn stood by the bed, holding the lamp, his eyes on the man, feeling again the paralyzing impact of shock just as he had a few minutes before when he had stood there.

Newt Kimmel had always been a tall, long-boned man, honed down to hard muscle by constant riding, but now he seemed to consist entirely of skin and bones. His face that had been deeply bronzed by wind and sun had faded to a ghastly gray.

As Horn turned to the bureau and set the lamp down, Rusty said: "Hell, he don't look like he'll live till morning."

"Dixie figured he was getting along," Horn said. "I reckon he'll be around for a while. Pretty damned tough, Newt is."

Horn pulled a rawhide-bottom chair to the head of the bed and sat down. Rusty dropped into a chair on the other side of the room. They sat there for a time, smoking, glancing occasionally at the sleeping man, while outside purple dusk left the valley and night moved in, a pressing blackness relieved only by faint star shine.

"I thought Dixie and Ruth would be along before now," Rusty said worriedly.

"Probably stayed in camp," Horn said.

There was silence again except for Kimmel's light breathing. Presently he stirred and opened his eyes. He stared at Horn a long moment, blinking, then he said: "Sometimes I see things when I wake up that ain't here, but damned if I don't believe you're really Jim Horn. Nobody else, either in this world or hell, could look as much like Jim as you do."

"It's me," Horn said, and held out a hand. "How are you, Newt?"

"Slicker'n goose grease." Kimmel pulled a skinny hand out from under the quilt and shook Horn's. "The only thing that's wrong is I just ain't worth a damn no more."

"Newt, meet Rusty Hancock from Ohio who wants to be a cowboy and has got more guts in him than any greenhorn I've ever seen before."

Pleased, Rusty stepped up and shook Kimmel's hand. "Glad to know you, Mister Kimmel. Don't let Jim fool you none. I've been scared ever since I left Fort Wallace."

Kimmel's thin lips stretched into a grin. "I sure cotton to an honest man. I'm scared, too, kid." He gripped Rusty's hand and dropped it. "What's more, I'm busted. When I get out of this damned bed, I start from scratch. Hear that, Jim? From scratch, and just last Christmas I bragged to Dixie I was the best fixed man in the territory."

"You still are."

"Like hell. Didn't Dixie tell you?"

"Sure, but Collier's dead. So's Dyer and Meeker. Another fellow they called Benson. Just Travis and Vance are left."

"And Travis is beat all to hell," Rusty said. "Jim done it."

The thin lips pulled back into the grin again. "That's

good news, but, as long as Vance is alive, I've got trouble. A slick one, that *hombre*. Anyhow, Clawhammer beef is scattered from here to breakfast. This valley is fifty miles long and ten wide, and most of them cows are up in the mountains by now. Why, even if I had a crew. . . ."

"We'll gather 'em for you, Newt."

"You and the kid? Jim, I used to tell you that your long hair would sap your brain and that's just what you've let it do."

"Listen to me, Newt. I've got quite a yarn." He told Kimmel about the colony and what had happened. He finished with: "You've always claimed all the valley when you never used a tenth of it. Well, these folks are here. They'll build a town. They've got the fixings . . . sawmill, gristmill, blacksmith shop, carpenter's tools. Everything. Horses and seed for farming. It'd be a good deal for both of you if you'd give each other a hand."

"So help me, Jim," Kimmel said angrily, "I'd have to be worse off than I am to throw in with a bunch of greenhorns. Anyhow, I haven't even got enough *dinero* to buy grub. . . ."

"I forgot one thing, Newt. Rusty here has fetched fifty thousand dollars in gold that he aims to invest in the valley. That means a loan to you. Now the settlers won't hurt you none. You've got all the grass on this side of the valley that you'll ever need, and you know it."

Kimmel was silent, fighting his natural dislike of settlers. Then he said: "Kid, if you've got that kind of money, you'll light out for the mines. . . ."

"No, I won't. I like this valley."

"Maybe you like Dixie."

Rusty glanced at Horn. Then he nodded. "Maybe I do."

"Well, Jim," Kimmel said bitterly, "I ain't in no shape to augur."

"I want your word that you'll help 'em," Horn said. "Sell 'em beef to eat this winter. Tell 'em what'll grow and what won't. Tell 'em where the best timber is. Best place for a dam so they can build a reservoir this summer when they can't do anything else but put up their cabins and maybe get in a late garden."

"Jim, I thought you said this wasn't a good valley for farming," Rusty said.

"It isn't, but there's a few grains that'll do all right. Hay. A few vegetables, but some things. . . ."

"What you're trying to say," Kimmel broke in, "is sooner or later the settlers will get around to raising cows."

"That's it," Horn admitted. "I always claimed there was room for fifty ranches if you had neighbors you could get along with."

Kimmel raised a hand and scratched the sharp point of his chin. "Yeah, I remember what you said. Well, I wouldn't be listening to you if Vance hadn't showed up with a bunch of toughs and put a slug into my brisket. All right, Jim, I'll make that deal if you'll run Clawhammer till I get on my feet. With a loan from the kid I can make out. . . ."

The beat of a horse's hoofs came to them. Whoever was coming was riding hard and fast. Horn ran out of the room to the front door. He stopped there, listening.

Rusty came up and would have gone on out if Horn had not held him back. He said: "Let's see who it is."

"It's trouble or. . . ."

"Sure, sure, but we might live longer if we see who's fetching it."

The horse was close now, a vague shape in the night. Then the rider pulled up under the cottonwoods, and Dixie cried out in a ragged voice: "Jim! Jim, you there?"

187

"You bet I'm here," Horn answered, and ran across the yard to her.

She swung out of her saddle and came to him, her hands gripping his arms. "I . . . I. . . ."

She began to cry, and Horn shook her roughly.

"What is it?"

"Vance got Ruth. We were on our way back and didn't know he was waiting for us. Tied me up. I just got loose a few minutes ago. Came as fast as I could."

"Where is he? What does he want with Ruth?"

"He's taking her to the Temple cabin. Said if you wanted her back, you'd come and get her. Said you had to be alone and you had to bring fifty thousand dollars." Her fingers dug into his arms. "He said if you tried any tricks, he'd take her over the mountains with him and you'd never see her again."

Chapter Four

Jim Horn had never been one to let emotion rule him. Like most men who had lived the kind of life he had, he had been forced by circumstances to accept danger philosophically, to realize that death comes but once and that, when a man chooses the frontier, it might come any time even when there is no reason to expect it. But the threat of danger to himself and to Ruth Morgan were two different things, and now fear was in him. It started deep in his belly and flowed upward into his chest until it hurt with dull, pressing pain.

Rusty lashed out at the girl. "Why in hell didn't you stay in camp . . . ?"

"Shut your mouth," Dixie flared. "You're just a wet-eared kid. Shut up now."

Whipped into silence, Rusty held his tongue.

Horn, shaking off the first shock, asked: "What about Travis?"

"I didn't see him. He might have been there, though. Vance pulled me off my horse, and I scratched him. He hit me and knocked me silly for a while. When I came to, he had me tied up."

Horn knew where Temple's cabin was, high up in the aspens on the slopes of the Sangre de Cristo range. He had been there many times when he had ridden for Clawhammer. Originally it had been a miner's shack, but Kimmel had worked it over until it was tight and sound and had used it for a summer cow camp.

Ruth would be comfortable and safe if it were any man but Clay Vance, but Vance could not be judged by the standards that applied to most Western men. Horn remembered how Vance had looked at Ruth the night he had ridden into the colonists' camp on the river and had called her "a fair woman to find in such a country." Horn was remembering, too, what Vance had said just before Horn's fight with Travis, about never having run into a woman he couldn't tame. Ruth had said: "You can't tame me." Those words, Horn thought, would be the kind of challenge Vance could not resist.

"Saddle my horse, Rusty," Horn said. "There's a lantern out there by the gate." He wheeled toward the house. "Come on, Dixie."

"Now what the hell are you . . . ?" Rusty began.

"Damn it, get a move on!" Horn called back. "Saddle your horse after I'm gone. You've got another ride to make."

Horn did not see if Rusty obeyed. Dixie caught up with him, asking: "What have you got in your head, Jim?"

"I'm going after her. Where's that Thirty-Two you used to have?"

"In my room, but it's too small. . . ."

"Get it. Fetch some string, too."

The instant they stepped into the house, Newt Kimmel called: "What is it?"

"Nothing to fret about," Horn answered. "Dixie's here."

"I'm all right, Dad," Dixie said, and ran into her room.

Horn lighted a lamp, took off his coat, and untied his

neckerchief. When Dixie brought the little pistol and string, he checked it, saw that the pistol was loaded, and looped the string through the trigger guard. "Drop it down my back," Horn told Dixie. "Tie the string so the gun will hang between my shoulder blades."

She obeyed, understanding then what he had in mind. Now, with the lamplight fully upon her face, he saw the dark bruise on the side of her jaw where Vance had struck her, and fury worked through him like an all-consuming fire. He held his silence, and, when she was done, he re-tied his neckerchief and slipped into his coat.

"How does it look?" Horn asked, stepping away from her. "See anything?"

She moved around him and shook her head. "It's not enough of a bulge to notice unless you're looking for it." She took a long breath. "But Vance will be looking, Jim. He was a gambler in Pueblo. He'll know all the tricks."

"Maybe he won't know this one," Horn said, and left the house.

Dixie stepped into the bedroom, said something to her father, and ran after Horn. When she caught up with him, she said: "Let me go with you, Jim. Rusty can stay with Dad."

"No."

"But Travis will probably be with Vance. I can shoot. Don't you remember how well I can shoot?"

But Horn ignored her question, and they went on to the corral.

Rusty had saddled Horn's gelding, and now he swung to Horn, bony face dark with worry. He said: "I'm going with you. Don't tell me I can't. Ruth means. . . ."

"I know how you feel, but this job's mine." Horn put a hand on the boy's shoulder. "When Morgan died, he said

191

he was giving Ruth's life into my hands. Now I've let this happen."

"Hell, it wasn't your fault."

"I pegged Vance wrong," Horn said grimly, "and that was my fault. I just didn't think far enough ahead. I should have because I saw the way he looked at her."

Rusty leaned against a corral post, shocked by a new fear that had not occurred to him before. He said in a low voice: "I didn't think about him wanting Ruth. Figured he was after my money."

"He wants Ruth *and* the money," Horn said, "and he wants to kill me."

"He tried to get Clawhammer . . . ," Dixie began.

"He's smart enough to know he can't have everything," Horn said. "Rusty, it's up to you whether you're gonna gamble with your *dinero*. If you're willing to, hike back to camp and get it. Fetch somebody to stay with Newt because Dixie will have to guide you. In case Vance drills me, Ruth'll need your help. If you work it right, you might be able to swap the *dinero* for Ruth."

"Sure, I'll get it, but I. . . ."

"It'll be daylight before we can get there," Dixie cut in.

Horn nodded. "He might pick you off before you get to the cabin, but I don't see any other way out of it. I made a deal with Newt, Dixie. If we get out of this, he'll still have Clawhammer."

"You didn't need to say that," Dixie said angrily. "We'll be along."

Horn stepped into the saddle. "I can't tell you how to play it because I don't know what'll happen after I get there, but maybe you'd better stay off the trail when you get into the aspens."

"We'll make out," Dixie said. "You take care of yourself, Jim."

"I'll sure as hell try," Horn said, and swung his horse upstream.

A mile up the creek, he crossed to a trail that followed the north rim of a steadily deepening cañon. It was country he had not seen for years, but he remembered it well. The time since he had last ridden this trail seemed very short, but the hours since he had brought the wagon train to the campsite at the mouth of Lost Creek had been an eternity. So much had happened during these last thirty-six hours.

It seemed to Jim Horn that his mind was something apart from him. It was fixed on Ruth and Clay Vance, and he found that he could make no plans. His racing thoughts were of mistakes and wrong judgments he had made. The colonists were not the children he had considered them. They would get along. During times of pressure there were some, like Carl Larson, who found in themselves a capacity for leadership they had not realized they possessed. But of all the colonists Rusty Hancock had proved the most surprising. The happenings of the last few days had thrust him from childhood into manhood, and he had accepted it.

Horn thought of Angus Morgan and knew he had been only partially right about the man. As Horn had told Ruth, her father had died a brave man, protecting those whose safety had been entrusted to him. At least, that was the way he would be remembered, and Horn was glad Ruth could hold this one good memory of him.

Now Horn thought of Morgan's saying that when a man lay dying, his values changed. Jim Horn wasn't dying, but the chances were good he would not be alive by morning, and, like Morgan's, his values had changed. There was no pulling and hauling in him now. He would have made the wrong decision that night when he had brought the wagon train into camp on the Arkansas. Now he knew what he wanted. If he lived, he would make the right decision.

The only mistake Horn condemned himself for was his wrong judgment of Clay Vance. He had not considered the possibility that Vance would strike at all of them through Ruth. Now, with the judgment of hindsight, it seemed the one thing he should have seen most clearly.

The miles dropped behind him with the hours. The country lifted sharply, and he could hear the pound of the creek far below him to his left. He was in the pines, the scraggly cedars below him. His horse's hoofs dropped softly into the pine needles, and the smell of timber, pungent in the high sharp air, was all about him.

At times, when he crossed small parks, he could see the sky, bright with stars. Then the pines closed in again and the darkness was complete. The climb grew so steep that the trail made long loops that put him a quarter of a mile from the cañon, but always it swung back to the rim. Black space was only a few feet from him then, and again he could hear the laughter of the creek, muffled by deep distance.

It was past midnight now. There was a possibility he would catch Vance and the girl before they reached the cabin. When he stopped to blow his horse, he listened attentively, but no sound of other horses came to him. He was certain Vance would be with the girl, but Travis was an unknown factor.

The more Horn thought about Ben Travis, the less certain he was about the man. He might have left the country, but, on the other hand, the desire to get square with Horn for the beating he had taken could be strong enough to make him stay. Either way, Horn would soon know.

Eventually, far above Clawhammer, the country leveled

off to a wide bench covered with aspens. The cañon swung south, and its walls were so precipitous that a crossing was impossible. It had been Kimmel's habit to drive Clawhammer's she-stuff to this bench for the summer and to take his steers to the other side of the creek. Now that he had reached the bench, Horn knew he was not far from Temple's cabin.

He reined up, listening. He thought he was close enough to the cabin to see a light if Vance and the girl had reached it, but there was no break in the darkness that pressed against the earth. Horn shivered and wished he had borrowed a sheepskin from Dixie, for the wind that drifted down from the high peaks above knifed into him with a penetration that was bone deep.

The first warning Horn had of another's presence was the faint smell of cigarette smoke. It would be Travis. Vance, Horn thought, was too smart to smoke if he planned a bushwhack death for Jim Horn. Horn drew his gun, thinking carefully about his next move. Probably Travis was still some distance up the trail. At least, Horn could not make out the glow of a cigarette. Or he could be quite near. Having heard the horse coming upgrade, he might have put his cigarette out, the smell of it lingering in the air momentarily.

The trick was to make Travis give his position away. Horn stepped out of saddle. Leaving his gelding ground hitched, he moved quickly to one side of the trail. There had been a faint *squeak* of leather, loud enough for Travis to hear if he was close. He might cut loose at the first sound he heard. On the other hand, he might be the kind who wanted Horn to know who was smoking him down. It was a common characteristic of men of his caliber—this perverted variety.

Horn waited, ears picking up no sound but the ceaseless whisper of the tiny aspen leaves above him. Then a light showed up the trail. Vance had brought a lamp to life in the cabin. Whether he had lighted it at that moment, or whether Horn had moved into position to see it was a question in his mind, but he could be reasonably certain that Vance and Ruth had reached the cabin and that Travis had been left to guard the trail.

It seemed logical that Vance and Travis intended to kill him and hoped to find the money in his saddlebags. This was an old game to Jim Horn, but this time the stakes were higher than they had ever been before.

Standing motionless in the blackness, Horn tried to reason out the move Travis would make, but he did not know Travis well enough to guess how the man would act. It had been his hope that Travis was the kind who would break and run after his licking, but it hadn't worked that way. Travis wanted revenge. Too, Vance had probably played on his greed by promising a cut from the money Horn had been told to bring. At any rate, he was here, but how close and what he would do when he located Horn were imponderables.

Horn's nerves tightened with the passing moments. He could not stand here doing nothing, not with Ruth in that cabin. He edged a few feet up the trail and stood with his back against an aspen trunk, listening. It seemed to Horn that his breathing was so loud it would warn Travis. Then he was aware of footsteps on the trail above him, faint but unmistakable. Horn knew he had succeeded in outwaiting Travis. The man had heard his horse and then, impatient with the delay, was moving down upon him.

Picking a cartridge from his belt, Horn tossed it to the other side of the trail. It hit a tree and bounced off, the noise exaggerated by the silence. The next instant Travis cut loose with a shotgun, a terrific blast that sounded like a cannon.

Travis was closer than Horn had thought. He threw a shot at the flash of powder flame, falling aside as Travis gave him the second barrel. The buckshot went over him, some splattering into the aspen trunk he had been leaning against. Flat on his stomach, Horn drove three more bullets at the spot where Travis had been standing, keeping them belly high and placing them a foot apart.

Horn rolled and came to his hands and knees, certain that he had hit Travis, for the man was groaning and threshing around in the dry leaves. There was one shell left in Horn's gun. He waited, holding his fire. Travis might have other loads for his shotgun, or at least he would have his belt gun, and there was no way of telling how hard he had been hit.

Again time ribboned out, each second dragging by like an hour. Slowly Horn worked toward the spot where he judged Travis was lying. His hand fell on a small limb. He picked it up and made a scratching sound as far from him as he could reach. At once Travis came into action, spraying the ground with lead. Horn used the last bullet in his gun. The echoes died, and for a short time Horn heard Travis's labored breathing. Then it stopped.

Horn could not take the chance of leaving a wounded man behind him. He lunged forward, and his outstretched hands found Travis's body. It was slack. There was no pulse.

Suddenly weak from the strain of these minutes, Horn came slowly to his feet. He reloaded his gun, fumbling in the darkness, and went back to his horse. He stepped into the saddle, and sat gripping the horn for a time. It seemed

to him he could not go on, that he had never been so completely tired in his life.

He passed out for a short time, slumped forward in the
saddle. When he straightened up with a start, it seemed to
him for one crazy moment that it was daylight and that
Ruth was with him. The image of her face was very real, the
dark eyes and black hair, the defiant chin with its dimple,
the freckles on her nose, the proud way she held her head.
He shook his head, fighting the weariness, and the illusion
was gone. The toughest part of his job was still to be done.

Travis was out of the way. Now there was only Clay
Vance, tricky and without conscience, Clay Vance who had
seen his dreams of power and wealth stolen from him by
Jim Horn. Horn put his horse up the trail, and soon came to
the cabin. The door was open, but there was no sign of
human presence.

Horn reined up before he reached the yellow pools of
lamplight falling into the clearing from the window and the
open door. He stepped down, gun palmed. He heard Ruth
cry out, a shrill, incoherent scream that brought him to the
cabin on the run. He lunged inside and saw Ruth tied in a
chair in the middle of the room. There was no sign of
Vance.

For an instant Horn stood just inside the door, motionless, trying to understand this and failing. Ruth was safe.
She was pale, her eyes wide and filled with terror, but she
was safe, and Vance was gone.

"Jim." Her faint whisper barely reached him. "Jim.
You're all right?"

"Sure I'm all right. Where's Vance?"

"I don't know. He was at the window a minute ago. Oh,
Jim, I've brought you nothing but trouble. If I'd only. . . ."

Then the door slammed shut. Vance's voice came clearly

from the window: "Stay inside, Horn, and don't go near the lamp, or I'll let the girl have it."

Horn wheeled toward the door. His first impulse was to go after Vance, but the man's words—"I'll let the girl have it."—were enough to hold him there. He turned back, eyes moving to the one dirty window in the south wall of the cabin. He could see nothing except the smudged panes of glass. The light was in Vance's favor. If he stood a few feet back from the window, Horn could not see him, but he could watch both Horn and Ruth.

"You're sure you're all right?" Horn asked. "Vance hasn't . . . ?"

She shook her head. "He's been as courteous as he could be under the circumstances. What does he want now?"

"Rusty's money. I was supposed to bring it."

"You didn't?"

"No. I came as soon as Dixie told me what had happened."

He crossed the room to her and cut the ropes that bound her to the chair, but when she tried to stand, there was no strength in her legs. Horn got hold of her arms and pulled her upright. She swayed against him and would have fallen if he had not held her.

"I'm sorry, Jim. I'm . . . I'm all in, I guess. Dad's being killed and riding up here with Vance and him telling me you were dead."

"We're still alive," he said softly. "We'll get out of this, some way."

She put her head against his shirt and stood that way, her body limp in his arms. She said, her voice muffled: "I'm such a weakling, Jim. I don't know why we ever came out. . . ."

He shook her roughly, his voice sharp: "Stop it. Stop it

now." Then he sensed that this was wrong, and he tightened his arms around her. "Listen, Ruth. We've all made some mistakes, but we'll pull out of this. I'm going to work for Newt Kimmel, and I'll stay here in the valley. He promised to help your bunch."

He felt the tension go out of her, and he hurried on: "Newt needs help, too, so it'll be a good deal for him and your outfit. He knows what the weather's like and what'll grow in the valley and where the best timber is. I'll get some of the young fellows and we'll gather his cattle and get 'em up here on summer range. The rest of the men can put in a dam so they can hold next spring's run-off. Might be they can get a little garden in before it's too late."

It was just talk, words designed to bring courage back into her. Horn did not know whether Vance was still at the window, but he could not take a chance on finding out. Ruth had had her moment of weakness. Now it was gone. She tipped her head back and looked at him, the sweet, familiar smile touching the corners of her mouth.

"You've changed, Jim," she whispered. "All this time I've been hoping you would. Dad said that when you tried something, you did it well, but he said you didn't have any responsibility. I knew he was wrong."

"Been a lot to change me," he said gravely. "I wouldn't have come along in the first place if you hadn't been with the wagon train. Didn't seem like I had any chance, so I didn't say anything."

"You had every chance," she whispered, "but you were the one who had to do something. I couldn't go to you and say . . . 'Jim, I love you.' Then, when you were going to leave the wagon train, I just couldn't let you go."

Funny, he thought. *Damned funny.* She'd been in love with him and he hadn't known. He'd thought she was out of his reach, and all the time she had been waiting for him. He had been blinded by his crazy fear of settling down, of taking on the responsibility of a family, of accepting the kind of life that was coming to the frontier.

"I'm not much," he said. "Not by the way folks like you figure a man, but . . . but. . . ." He searched for words and, failing to find them, blurted: "There's some things I can do, but saying a thing isn't one of 'em. Will you marry me?"

"Yes, Jim, if you think I'll do."

"You just bet you'll do," he said quickly. "You've got something inside you that all hell can't take out."

"I'll try, Jim," she breathed. "I'll try awfully hard."

He kissed her, her arms tightly around him, and she was slow to give up his lips. It was crazy, kissing her at a time like this. He might die within the hour, or within the minute, and here they were, talking about their future. Perhaps these few minutes together would be all they would ever have, and he sensed that she was as much aware of this as he was. If it had not been this way, he might never have found the courage to ask her to marry him.

The door opened, and Horn knew that Vance had come in. The man had not stayed at the window, but Horn did not regret the chance he had missed. Ruth's safety was the one thing he could not gamble with.

"Make the most of it," Vance said as if amused. "I always say that a man should take advantage of opportunity when it comes because it doesn't come very often."

Ruth stepped back, and Horn turned around to face the gambler. Vance was not as immaculate as he had been. A long, bloody slash on one cheek showed where Dixie had scratched him, his clothes were dirty, his eyes bloodshot, and he needed a shave. He held a gun in his hand, and Horn, giving him a close study, sensed that Clay Vance had been pushed as far as he could be, that it would take very little to make him commit murder.

"Looks like you're still hanging onto your opportunity," Horn said.

"You're damned right I am. I'm a gambler, mister, and any gambler knows that the only way to win is to keep the odds balanced in his favor." He motioned for Horn to step back. "Take off your gun belt and drop it. You've been nothing but bad luck to me from the first minute I saw you. Now I aim to kill you."

Horn moved back, unbuckled his belt, and let it drop. He said: "You'll lose your last chance of getting your hands on Rusty's money if you do."

"That's the only reason I haven't drilled you before." Vance jabbed a finger toward the bunk. "Get over there and sit down." When Horn obeyed, Vance nodded at Ruth. "Sit down where you were."

Horn sat motionlessly on the bunk, the gun that Dixie had given him making a small pressure against his back. He asked: "What do you want the most, Vance?"

"The *dinero*. Didn't the Kimmel girl tell you to bring it?"

"She told me all right," Horn answered.

"I just had a look in your saddlebags, and it isn't there. If you think coming up here empty-handed will save your hide, you're loco."

Horn understood now why Vance had not prevented his cutting Ruth's ropes. He had left the window to examine Horn's saddlebags. Horn glanced at Ruth. She sat on the edge of her chair like a bird about to take wing. He shook his head at her, hoping to make her understand that a wild move of any kind would finish their slim chance of getting out of this.

"Let's have a little palaver, Vance." Horn drew tobacco

and paper from a pocket and rolled a smoke. "You're making one mistake. Rusty won't hand the *dinero* over to you unless Ruth and me are both alive."

"What makes you think he'll ever hand it over to me?"

"I headed up the creek as soon as Dixie told me what had happened. I sent Rusty back to camp to get the gold."

"Hell, he'll never find this cabin."

"Dixie is coming with him."

"And I suppose he'll fetch the greenhorns along." Vance shook his head. "No good, Horn. I told the Kimmel girl I'd take Ruth and leave the country if you didn't bring it. That's what I'll do, and I don't aim to leave you behind to follow me."

Vance's lips tightened. He thumbed the hammer of his gun, and for a moment Horn thought it would be finished then. It would have been if Ruth had not risen.

"Mister Vance, if you pull the trigger, you might as well kill me," Ruth said, "but if you let him live, I'll go with you. You have only my word for it, but it should be enough. I love Jim. Try to understand that, Mister Vance. I never knew before what it was to love a man, but I do now. Whatever I have to give, I'll give it because of him."

Vance shook his head. "It isn't enough. If I leave Horn alive, he'll trail me from here to hell-an'-gone. I don't want to keep looking over my shoulder the rest of my life."

She had won a moment's reprieve. Horn began talking again to gain more time. He said: "When I left Clawhammer, I told Rusty there were three things you wanted, the money and Ruth and my life. That right?"

"Very right."

"Well, if you're smart, you'll get the *dinero* for sure and you might wind up with all three."

"I aim to." Vance studied Horn a moment. "Just how do

you figure I ought to be smart?"

"Rusty and Dixie will be here about dawn. They'll have the *dinero,* but if Ruth or me aren't alive, they won't make any bargain with you."

Vance was silent a moment, considering that. He was too much of a gambler to let his thoughts or feelings show in his face, but Horn was reasonably sure that greed was the most powerful motive in his make-up. That meant there was a chance.

"So you're giving me till dawn to decide what to do with you," Vance said.

"I'm saying you'd be smart to keep me alive till dawn. Take a look at it, Vance. You can't take Ruth back down the mountain or you'll run into the greenhorns and they'll hang you higher'n hell. You can't take her over the mountains into the San Luis Valley. Nobody's ever gone over from here. You'd better make the best deal you can."

"I'll make my own deal," Vance said harshly. "To hell with your advice."

"You aren't as smart as I figured you were," Horn said as if disappointed.

"I'll get her over the mountains, all right," Vance said, "but I want the *dinero,* too. I've been looking for a stake like that all my life." His face turned ugly. "I had my hands on a big thing here, and you fixed it. Damn you, Horn, I've got a notion to plug you where you sit."

"But you've got a better notion. Once you get to the mining camps with fifty thousand in gold, you can have your own saloon and gambling place, and you'll be fixed for life. I think you'll wait, friend."

Vance sat down on a bench near the door, his gun still on Horn. Watching him, Horn had the feeling that his talk was wasted. Vance hated him so much that killing wasn't enough. The gambler wanted to keep him talking and hoping while all the time he planned to kill him when it suited his whim.

Vance was certain he could outwit Rusty and Dixie when they came. Or if they brought a band of settlers, he was confident that Ruth gave him all the bargaining power he needed. Now he was enjoying this power to take life with the sadistic satisfaction of a cat that permits a mouse to live while it is held prisoner by his claws.

Ruth was still standing in front of her chair, scornful eyes on Vance. She said: "You're no part of a man. Why don't you tell us what you plan to do?"

"All right," Vance murmured. "I'll beef your man, you'll go with me, and I'll get the *dinero*. Your luck's run out. I don't give a damn about Travis. He wanted to leave the country after he got that licking today. Only way I could hold him was to promise to fetch Horn up here which I did."

"Your luck's run thin, too," Horn said. "Travis is dead."

"That was his luck, not mine. I always played a lone hand till I got into this deal, and from now on I'm playing it that way."

"How'd you get lined up with Webb?" Horn asked.

"Met him on Cherry Creek in the early days," Vance said. "He was broke when he went back to Ohio. I ran into him in Pueblo when he came out here to spot a place for the colony. He told me young Hancock would be along with a pile of *dinero*, so we rigged the whole deal. I knew about this valley and about Clawhammer, and I told him I'd have Newt Kimmel whittled down to size. I did, too."

Ruth moved to the table. "We're wasting time. Let Jim go. I told you I'd go with you willingly if you did. You'll need some luck, Mister Vance, and I'll bring it to you."

"I make my own luck," he said. "You'll go with me regardless of your long-haired friend."

"Fifty thousand is quite a chunk of luck," Horn said.

"I told you I'd have that, too." Vance leaned forward, anticipation showing in his face. "Ruth's right about wasting time. Might as well finish this."

Horn untied his handkerchief and dropped it on the bunk. He had played for time, hoping for a break that had not come, and he had gained all he could. He thought of his drifting years when he had ridden aimlessly, searching for something he had never identified. Now he had found it. He had every reason to live, and he had only seconds. He could jerk at the string around his neck and try to get hold of Dixie's gun, but he would die. The break had not come.

There were these few seconds of silence, and Vance was squeezing all the pleasure from them he could. The hammer of his gun was back and his finger was tightening on the trigger. Horn tensed, trying to guess the exact second when Vance would fire. He could go sideways off the bunk and make his try for the little gun. If he had any luck, he might make Vance miss one shot, but that still wouldn't buy the time he needed.

"Mister Vance," Ruth said, "I have something to say."

She stood very straight beside the table, her head held in the proud way that Horn liked, her chin thrust defiantly at Vance.

The gambler relaxed. "Well?"

"I made an offer," Ruth said. "You are so silly that you would rather kill a man you hate than take it, or perhaps you're relying too much on your luck. But either way, I'll make you a promise. There will come a time when I'll have a chance to kill you, and I will do it."

Vance's eyes glittered. "I like that. I told you I had never found a woman I couldn't tame. You said I couldn't tame you, but I will. It'll take time, but I'll do it."

"That was a bet I told you you'd lose. We'll see as to that, but now I have the right to kiss Jim good bye, and I'm taking it."

She swung around and walked to the bunk, heels *clicking* against the rough plank floor. If there was any fear in her, Horn could see no trace of it. She leaned over him, put her arms around him. She whispered: "Don't use your gun till you have the right chance." Then she kissed him, and drew away, her eyes lingering on his face as if storing the picture of it in her memory, as she backed to the table.

"I've learned a good many things since we left Fort Wallace, Mister Vance," Ruth said in a cool, distant voice. "I've seen things I never would have believed if I had been told about them when we were in Ohio, but the most unbelievable thing I've seen is you."

She leaned forward, her hands palm down on the table. Vance looked at her, not knowing how to take what she'd said. He asked: "What do you mean by that?"

"I just didn't think there was anything like you," she said. "I didn't suppose any human was capable of shooting down a man in cold blood the way you propose to do with Jim. You'd put a skunk to shame, Mister Vance. You'd make the stripe fade right off his back."

"That talk won't get you anywhere." Vance's lips were white with the sudden fury that burned through him. "You'll damned soon find that out."

Vance rose and stepped toward Horn, increasing the pressure against the trigger. As he took the step, Ruth snatched up the lamp and threw it at him. Horn dived off the bunk just as Vance's gun roared, the sound like nearby thunder in the small cabin.

Vance had not been watching Ruth; he had expected nothing from her. His shot, instead of drilling Horn through the chest, merely burned along Horn's back like the passing tip of a red-hot iron. Vance squalled like a hurt animal as he lunged forward and fell. The coal oil from the broken lamp was already flaming when Horn pulled out his hidden gun and got a firm grip on it.

Vance's second shot was unintentional, the reflex action of a panicky man scrambling frantically to get clear of the fire that was rushing up the side of the cabin wall and spreading across the rough floor.

Horn, kneeling in front of the bunk, tilted his gun upward at Vance and squeezed the trigger twice, the bark of the little pistol cracking into the booming echoes of Vance's big revolver. Horn's first bullet got the gambler through the neck, the second drove into his brain. He was dead when he plunged forward on his face, with flames licking at his clothes.

Ruth stood, frozen, beside the table. Horn picked her up and, slapping his hat over her face, plunged through the fire. There was a moment when the flames were all around them, a thousand leaping red devils clutching at them, then they were outside and sucking the chill mountain air into their lungs.

Horn stumbled on until he was away from the intense heat of the fire. He put Ruth down, using his hat to slap at the smoldering patches on her skirt. The smell of his own singed hair was strong in his nostrils, and he wiped a hand across his smudged, scorched face. Relief brought a trembling weakness to him. Another thirty seconds would have been too late.

"Jim, you're. . . ."

"I'm all right. Buckskin doesn't burn easy. Anyhow, a

little frying is nothing after what we just missed."

"Vance will burn to death," the girl cried. "Even a man like that doesn't deserve. . . ."

"He's already dead. I've got a notion the devil's fixed up a fire for him that's gonna last a long time."

The whole cabin was blazing now. Stumbling with weariness, Horn led Ruth into the aspens. He sat down with his back against a tree trunk. She dropped to the ground beside him and turned to watch the flames.

"Funny about men like that," she said. "In one way he was like Dad. So sure of himself that he made a mistake that killed him."

"How'd you know I had a gun?"

"I felt it the first time I kissed you. When you first came into the cabin and untied me." She took a long, ragged breath, shuddering. "I never want to go through anything like that again. Seems queer he didn't search you."

"I reckon he didn't care whether I had a gun or not. He had the drop on me, and he sure didn't count on you taking chips in the game."

The first opalescent light of dawn was showing in the eastern sky. Rusty and Dixie would be along soon. Horn reached out and took Ruth's hands. He said: "Your dad and Rusty figured I was too much Indian to marry you. Rusty's notions have changed some, I reckon, but they were about half right."

"No they weren't," she said quickly. "It's going to be different now, Jim. Don't you see? This whole country is changing. Towns and railroads and. . . ."

"That's what I'm trying to say," he broke in. "The trouble's been that I knew Jim Bridger and Kit Carson, and some of the others, and I liked their kind of life. Now I've got sense enough to see I was loco. I've just been playacting."

She was leaning forward, trying to see his face. "Jim, I would never want to hold a man if he didn't love me the way I did him."

"I don't mean that. It's just that maybe I'll get tired of living like other white men do and start out again."

"I'll go with you," she said quickly. "I had a lot to do with persuading Dad to come out here. Maybe I'm half Indian myself. Or Gypsy or something."

"Well, then, we'll get along. I'm not saying this very well, but there's one thing I will do. I'll get a hair cut."

She laughed softly. "I understand better than you think I do. It's been a sort of symbol with you, but. . . ."

Afterwards he wished he'd waited a few seconds before kissing her. She never could remember what she was going to say.

About the Author

Wayne D. Overholser won three Spur Awards from the Western Writers of America and has a long list of fine Western titles to his credit. He was born in Pomeroy, Washington, and attended the University of Montana, University of Oregon, and the University of Southern California before becoming a public schoolteacher and principal in various Oregon communities. He began writing for Western pulp magazines in 1936 and within a couple of years was a regular contributor to Street & Smith's *Western Story Magazine* and Fiction House's *Lariat Story Magazine*. *Buckaroo's Code* (1947) was his first Western novel and remains one of his best. In the 1950s and 1960s, having retired from academic work to concentrate on writing, he would publish as many as four books a year under his own name or a pseudonym, most prominently as Joseph Wayne. *The Violent Land* (1954), *The Lone Deputy* (1957), *The Bitter Night* (1961), and *Riders of the Sundowns* (1997) are among the finest of the Overholser titles. *The Sweet and Bitter Land* (1950), *Bunch Grass* (1955), and *Land of Promises* (1962) are among the best Joseph Wayne titles, and *Law Man* (1953) is a most rewarding novel under the pseudonym Lee Leighton. Overholser's Western novels, whatever the byline, are based on a solid knowledge of the history and customs of the 19th-

Century West, particularly when set in his two favorite Western states, Oregon and Colorado. Many of his novels are first-person narratives, a technique that tends to bring an added dimension of vividness to the frontier experiences of his narrators and frequently, as in *Cast a Long Shadow* (1957), the female characters one encounters are among the most memorable. He wrote his numerous novels with a consistent skill and an uncommon sensitivity to the depths of human character. Almost invariably, his stories weave a spell of their own with their scenes and images of social and economic forces often in conflict and the diverse ways of life and personalities that made the American Western frontier so unique a time and place in human history. *Wild Horse River* will be his next **Five Star Western**.

The employees of Five Star hope you have enjoyed this book. All our books are made to last. Other Five Star books are available at your library, through selected bookstores, or directly from us.

For information about titles, please call:

(800) 223-1244

or visit our Web site at:

www.gale.com/fivestar

To share your comments, please write:

Publisher
Five Star
295 Kennedy Memorial Drive
Waterville, ME 04901